ii

JANETTA FUDGE-MESSMER

It's a Mystery Birds

By Janetta Fudge-Messmer

Copyright © **2021**
Written by: Janetta -Messmer
Published by: Gordian Books, a division of Winged Publications

This book is a work of fiction. Names, characters, places, and incidents are the product of the author's imagination and are used fictitiously. Any resemblance to actual events, locales, or persons, living or dead, is coincidental.

No part of this book may be copied or distributed without the author's consent.

ISBN: 9798870918488

ACKNOWLEDGEMENTS:

Thank you to my editors. You stretched me. You made me think. You made the book better with all your red marks. ☺ Blessings to all of you. I also have to thank the Lord for giving me the stick-to-itiveness on this novel. I don't know how many times I wanted to put it away, but He helped me persevere to the finish line.

THE HOLY BIBLE, NEW INTERNATIONAL VERSIONS®, NIV® Copyright © 1873, 1978, 1984, 2011 by Biblica, Inc.(TM) Used by permission. All rights reserved worldwide.

CHAPTER ONE

"Ben, are you sure you and the pooch will be okay at the campground without me? I don't have to attend the writer's conference." Betsy's insides danced around like hula dancers at a Friday-night luau.

"Hon, we'll be fine. Once you walk inside, we'll be a mere memory. When your writer friends from Houston arrive, they and the conference will keep you occupied for the next three days."

"Fine, I'll go." Bets collected her belongings. "I'll text you what room Debbie and I are in…in case you—"

"In case of what? You'll be fine. Now go, or I'm driving off with you still in the truck. Oh, but I can't. You paid good money to attend. Here, let me get the door to aid in your sooner-than-later departure."

Her hubby's laughter, antics opening her door, and helping her out of their vehicle increased her angst. "Ben, I'm having a traumatic moment, and you're making jokes. I'm going because my editor said, "You have to make an appearance with your first book."

"And…"

"And, Dillon McCloud is here. I'm dying to meet this new-to-me author." Betsy swooned over the famous mystery writer. "Ben, her ability to weave words leaves me feeling like a kindergartener wrote my novel."

"Bets, you're in your head again. Get out of it. Listen to the verse the Lord gave you in Philippians. 'Whatever is true, whatever is noble. You know the rest.'" He smiled at her, but his slightly miffed expression showed his true feelings.

"You're right, Benjamin Stevenson. And it's time for me to scoot. Love ya!"

Ben returned to the truck and lowered the side window. "Hon, don't forget to talk to Mr. Pickle about your idea. He's sure to agree since it's the premise of your second book. And, when writers find out about it – they'll clamor to enter a contest to win a trip in our RV."

"Will do." Betsy turned toward the hotel but realized three steps into her journey, she'd forgotten to wave goodbye to her hubby. "No worries. Ben understands Dillon McCloud is inside this hotel, and I have to get her autograph."

At that moment, the automatic doors opened, allowing Betsy and the other guests to enter the hotel. The lobby's opulence contrasted with the casual clothing all around, including her own. *Lord, even if going to this conference scares the wits out of me – I'm here to learn.*

Weeks earlier, without thinking or praying about it, Bets had signed up for the conference and every session of Dillon's. Then reality hit. She'd have to tell Ben they'd be making a trip to Daytona since he confirmed their bank balance daily. He'd see the extra charges.

When she filled him in, he'd taken the news better than she'd imagined. "Larry can handle supervising the roofers. I'm glad you're surrounding yourself with like-minded people. Let's get packing. Oh, we don't have to pack. We carry our belongings with us."

Betsy made her next phone call to her best friend and RVing buddy, Rose Wilford. The same person who also adored Dillon's books. Bets would act as if it wasn't a big deal that she'd be hobnobbing with a New York Times bestselling author at the conference.

Their conversation proceeded as she expected. Nothing Betsy's dearest friend said sounded like the English language. "Rosie, take a breath. Larry, are you there if she keels over?"

"I'm fanning her as we speak."

And when Ben and Betsy took off that morning for Daytona – Rosie came out to send them off. As she hugged them, she said, "I'm giving you extra, super-duper ones, so you don't forget me."

Betsy wheeled her suitcase to the front desk of the hotel, and grinned. *How could I ever forget you, Mrs. Wilford? Oh, and I better call her when I get to my room.*

~~~

Betsy flopped on the king bed after checking in and listened to her friend. When Rose's words slowed, she jumped in, "If I meet Dillon McCloud, I may get to say two words to her while she's signing copies of her books for us. I'll try to get a picture of her and me together."

"You better, and you know if the repairs on Sassy Second *Two's* roof weren't going on, I'd be there with you."

"And you'd come with me to a writer's

conference...why?"

"I'm not answering it because our second-hand store is Larry and my first priority. You've heard, 'God's got the whole world in his hands?' Right now, He and the helpers He sent are finishing up the job in the next few days. No more leaks to ruin any more of our donations."

"Amen! And I'm guessing Everly and Douglas are thrilled to be back to work at the store."

"They are, and their wedding plans are coming along as well. But enough about us in Florida, what other writerly things will you be doing? Oh, and is it raining where you are? I heard it's a downpour in Houston where Debbie's coming from."

"We had rain all the way here." Betsy's head still hurt from the squeaking of the wiper blades. "About my plans, I'll attend classes tomorrow. Tonight, I'm signing my books. I hope the box arrived, or the five copies I have in my purse will have to suffice."

"Betsy, I have a grand idea. Dillon will have a table where she's signing books. How about you ask her if you can share her space? You have one book, and it doesn't take up much room."

"Rosebud, I have to go. I promise I'll call you later."

Betsy unpacked and texted Ben with the room information. The bed beckoned her again, but she overcame the urge to nap. Instead, she surveyed her clothes in the closet and verified nothing needed ironing.

And she checked through her pouch where she'd stuck her business cards and rack cards. "Yes, they're still in the same place I put them this morn—" Her phone rang, and a glance at the screen prompted her to yell, "Debbie, please tell me you're at the hotel?"

"I wish I could, but the airline canceled our flights

from Houston today due to thunderstorms. We'll give it another shot tomorrow."

She stared at the phone. "Are my ears plugged? I thought you said you weren't on a plane, flying to Daytona."

"That's sort of what I said. Maybe the rain, which is creeping up my sidewalk, is garbling our connection. It's crazy, Bets, but I've never seen so much water in such a short time. Hope to see you tomorrow, but I doubt it."

"I'll pray the rain ends soon and the gang can get here." Betsy clicked off her phone and texted Ben the latest news. He called a second later. Instead of "Hello," she said, "So much for catching up with my Texas buds."

~~~

Betsy changed into her business/casual outfit at 6:00 and headed to the elevators at the end of her floor. She pushed the button, and the door opened, revealing Dillon McCloud and another lady.

The mystery writer spoke first, "Hello there. Come on in and tell me what brings you here this weekend? I presume you're here for the writer's conference?" Her Southern accent drifted out into the hallway where Betsy stood.

Seconds ticked by before her feet made forward progress, but words stayed stuck in her throat. That was until she tripped, then out came, "I'm taking all of your classes, but it looks like I should have signed up for one on how to enter glass enclosures with a famous author inside."

Snickers erupted, but as the elevator door closed, Dillon came and stood next to Betsy. "Honey, I'm no more important than the squished bug on that glass wall. You settle yourself down, and no fussing over me. You know my name. What's yours?"

Betsy heard Barry Manilow's quip in her head from years ago. At one of his concerts, he called a woman to the stage and asked if she knew, "Can't Smile Without You." Her reply, "I did before you called me up here." At that very moment, Bets concurred with the woman at the concert. *What is my name?*

"It's not hard. Dig in your purse and show me your driver's license."

Bets regained her composure after a long, cleansing breath. "My name is Betsy Stevenson."

"I'm so glad to meet you. This is Arlene Peterson, my agent."

The Arlene Peterson. Goodness and mercy all the days of my life!

"Betsy, you do know, my bug sits next to Dillon's on the wall over there." The elevator stopped on the first floor, and the doors opened. "Come see us at the book signing. We'll have Dillon's latest book waiting for you. It's not even in the bookstore yet. Hope to see you."

The two women exited the elevator arm in arm, and Betsy concluded if a boat ventured into the open elevator, they'd be able to park in the gaping hole she called her mouth. "I'm dreaming and don't want to wake up."

An older gentleman walked in and said, "It's not a dream, but if you don't exit, the doors will close, and you'll be going back up again."

Bets thanked the man and hurried out. A sign pointed her to a room where they'd hold the book signing. She entered the double doors and spotted a flowered bench, and sat down. "Rose is going to lose all sense of smell and taste when I tell her about my chance meeting."

She sent her a text, but no response came. Her friend had either lost her phone, left it at their RV, or Betsy's news triggered her to lose consciousness. "Or Rosie's mad and is no longer talking to me."

Bets stashed her phone and spied Dillon and Arlene across the large room. The famous author appeared to motion to someone, but they must not have gotten the message because her arm movements continued. It finally hit her – s*he's telling me to come over.*

As offhanded as her jubilance allowed, Betsy acknowledged her with hand gestures of her own. However, they resembled signs she gave Ben when he attempted to back into an RV site—unrecognizable to the human eye, and today, to a famous author and her agent.

The two ladies made it clear her moves left them in the dark. So to clear it up, Betsy summoned the courage to walk over and explain. However, a dozen other authors blocked her way, and it appeared the opportunity had passed. *Maybe later.*

She retreated and searched for her table. When she found it, her delivered books sat behind the chair. Betsy tore the tape off of the box and brought out a half dozen copies. Arranging them gave her a sense of accomplishment. *Lord, you and I did this together.*

A scan around the room reminded her she needed to find her plastic stand and sack of candy she'd brought. Betsy hunted in her bag and found both, along with the pouch she'd put her stash of rack cards and business cards.

Bets placed her copy of *Always Enjoy the Journey,* her single offering, on the stand and stacked another six behind it. The candies, she scattered around them. "People always want something sweet…and they also want to see more books. One novel won't cut it."

The tiny space Betsy's books equaled three and a half feet. The rest of the table lay bare. She prayed that the hotel had installed a retractable roof, and it would open, and decorations would fall from it, filling the rest of the white tablecloth.

Bets laughed at the absurdity of her deliberation but knew if Rosie occupied the chair next to her, she'd have her lie on the table and point at her single contribution to the literary world.

Her thoughts again amused her, and it prompted another glimpse at her phone – still no reply from Rosie. Betsy stuck it away in her pocket and headed to the other side of the enormous room, hoping to find Dillon's table.

A large sign in the middle of the room announced Dillon's book signing. It and people weaving through the temporary maze jiggled Betsy's memory about the organizers starting the mystery writer's event an hour earlier than the rest.

Betsy stood in line and waited her turn…until Arlene Peterson approached her. "Dillon said for you to bring your books to her table. She loves to help out new authors. Come along, she'll make room for you."

"No, I'm fine where I'm at." But, unfortunately, Betsy's blasé statement didn't match the response of her sweat glands. Instead, they flowed like the Mississippi after the rainy season. "Arlene, my table is just fine. But please thank her for me."

"If you're sure. But when Dillon and—"

"Sorry to interrupt, Arlene, but I've been looking for my client." Andrew Pickle stepped up next to them. "Will you excuse us?"

"Sure." Dillon's agent glanced her way. "Betsy, when

we finish, we'll come see you at your table."

"And it's time for us to get to it." Betsy's editor held the rope up, and she ducked under it. He ushered her to her table, which now included a young woman with an adorable pixie haircut.

"Amy Spencer, I'd like you to meet Betsy Stevenson. She writes comedy, and from her reviews – she keeps her readers laughing. Amy's brand new, and her first book is a fantasy. Now it's time for me to check on my other authors and for you to get set up."

Mr. Pickle left, and Bets turned to her tablemate. "It's nice to meet you. I thought I'd be by myself. If there's anything I can help you with, let me know." *Other than giving you the whole table and escaping with my books to sell them at Dillon's table.*

"I hope you're into decorating. I brought along two trash bags full of all kinds of colorful streamers and confetti. It's enough to cover every table in the room if they're into that sort of thing."

She'd asked for decorations to fall from the ceiling, but Betsy never imagined the magnitude sitting in front of her. How did she miss a person carrying in two gargantuan bags? But there wasn't time to ponder since her editor returned to their table.

"Betsy, I wanted to tell you I'm sorry for taking you away from Dillon's book signing."

Her agent's apology impressed her, and she grinned. "It's okay, Mr. Pickle. There's always tomorrow."

"Yes, tomorrow. Gotta run. Oh, and please call me Andrew. No need for formalities since we work together. Have fun, and I'll check in on you two later."

"Thanks, Andrew." The urge to laugh and cry at the same time came close to overwhelming Betsy. *So much for hanging out with a New York Times bestselling author. No one is going to believe me when I tell them what happened. Especially Ros—"*

"Wait until you see this charmer, Betsy."

She wanted to ignore Amy's exuberance, but the item she held made of cardboard caught her attention. Her tablemate opened the tabs on the back, and the cutout grew into a three-dimensional stack of books with a person sitting on top.

"I'm speechless." *And, did I mention the showpiece measures three feet tall?*

Amy centered it on the table. "Don't you love it?"

"Well, it's quite the showstopper."

"I agree. Attracting attention is what I had in mind. And, Betsy, the teal blues and grays in it work with your book cover too."

"They do. It certainly makes our table stand out." Betsy's earlier disappointment vanished, and she hollered, "Amy, hand me the biggest bag of confetti you brought? I feel a party coming on!"

"You're my kind of girl. Go forth and glitter."

When Bets finished flinging sparkly stuff on their table and the adjoining ones, she came back and found Amy in tears, twisting a tissue between her fingers. Pieces of it dropped on the carpet, creating a sizeable pile.

She hurried over to her. "Amy, I know how you feel. I've been there. You're experiencing the newbie-book-signing jitters. After you sign your first book, you'll feel as if you've reached the summit of Mount Everest. Then, you'll be a pro."

"Why would anyone buy my book?" The new author wiped her nose with the used Kleenex. "Betsy, why am

I here? I'm not an author." The twenty-something author slapped her novel. "These words are junk."

"Our editor already gave you this speech." Betsy stopped for a moment as Andrew Pickle approached their table, then she continued. "Amy, remember he always tells his authors. 'Linnstrom-Peterson Publishing prints books—'"

"Yes, books readers want to read, and our prayer is that they point them toward the Lord." Andrew touched the centerpiece. "Amy, you've got this. And with this elaborate addition to your table – I predict business will be booming."

~~~

Betsy gathered her remaining books after another successful book signing. She peeked at Amy, and she glowed. *Thank You, Lord, for giving both of us a stupendous night and helping my newest friend relax.*

"How about we drop our books in my room and go get a latte?"

After a quick peek at Dillon's table – still overflowing with fans, Betsy concurred, "Amy, that sounds wonderful. We deserve a goodie too."

While they walked down the hall to the café, Betsy shared her elevator story. "I've been embarrassed on other occasions, but this one tops my list of faux pas." Bets heard the young woman's laughter, and at the end of it, a tiny snort escaped.

"Amy, my friend, Rose, doesn't have children, but the last noise you made is exactly like hers. I wish she'd been here to meet you, but she's in Fort Myers. She'd have given you the biggest hug you've ever encountered."

Her eyes brightened. "I live in Naples. When we get back, let's arrange to meet."

They chatted about their writing journey while sipping their coffee. Betsy nibbled on a slice of pumpkin bread. In between bites, she shared her on-the-road experiences. "They gave me tons of fodder for my novel. I'm amazed at what I've overheard people say in public. My advice, carry a pad of paper with you at all times."

"I will."

"And, I hate to cut this short, but it's 9:45. This lady has had a long day. I'll swing by your room in the morning and get my books."

"Thanks for tonight, and for you and Mr. Pickle, oh I mean, Andrew, talking me off the ledge."

"Anytime. We writers have to stick together." Betsy hugged her friend. "Bye."

On the way to her room, she remembered she hadn't spoken to Dillon about not sharing her table. *I'll catch her tomorrow.* She strolled to the elevator and punched the button for her floor.

As she walked the short distance to her room, Betsy relived the evening's festivities. She unlocked the door without much thought, and it flung open to reveal the last person she expected. Rose Wilford stood in front of her with her arms opened wide.

"I'd ask you where you've been, but you're with your peeps who don't pay one lick of attention to the time. Come here and hug your friend."

Dumbstruck, Betsy stayed put. "What are you doing here, and how did you get in my room?"

"Funny how far a little charm will get you. Now, where is Dillon McCloud? I'm dying to meet her."

Betsy chuckled. "There's a good possibility she's in her bed snoozing, which I'd like to do." She lay her purse and computer on the chair, gave her friend a huge hug, and then headed to her bed. "But I'm still perplexed how you convinced the front desk to let you in here."

Rosie punched at the pillows on the other king bed and settled into them. "After reading your text about Debbie not showing up, I immediately told Larry, "I'm taking the Minnie Winnie and driving up to Daytona. So here I am."

"Thought your store, and the need for a new roof, ranked higher than me?"

"Not when my best bud is all alone in a hotel room. I had to lend my moral support in such a dire situation."

Betsy rotated to face her friend on the other bed. "Rosebud, this tops all of your other concocted stories. The truth is – you wanted a glimpse of Dillon McCloud and not just in a photo I'd bring home."

"You are absolutely right. Nothing is better than the real thing."

~~~

Betsy brushed her teeth the following morning and still wondered why Rosie drove the RV instead of their little car. But last night, after all her excitement with Dillon and Amy at the book signing, she'd fallen asleep while her best friend kept on chattering.

She came out of the bathroom and focused on Rosie. "You do know I have classes all day. And you're aware you cannot come to any of them. You haven't paid. You cannot sneak in. Am I clear on this?"

"I don't want to say you rolled out of the wrong side of the bed...but Miss Smarty Pants doesn't suit you this early in the morning. Also, the front of your shirt has toothpaste dripping off of it."

"Great." Bets changed into another top and left Rose to fend for herself. On her way to Dillon's class, her phone alerted her of a text. Debbie's message said, "PLANES STILL GROUNDED IN HOUSTON!!! WE'RE STUCK HERE!!!"

Betsy replied, "I'll miss you and your smiling faces." She pocketed her phone and entered the classroom. The mystery writer and her agent sat at a table facing the front wall. Betsy picked a seat in the third row to not appear as an overzealous fan or an eavesdropper.

She modified the placement of her computer to find the most comfortable spot, and her eyes beheld the bottom toolbar. *Low battery? The cord must have jiggled out when I dropped my bag on the chair last night.*

While she unwrapped her cord, Bets looked around for an outlet on the wall. None were available at the end of the row she'd chosen. But she'd arrived in plenty of time to find one in the row behind her original seat and plugged in. It didn't work.

"Honey, not to use a cliché, but do you have ants in your pants?" Dillon McCloud stood next to Betsy at the non-working outlet. "If you will give me the plug, I'll see if the one next to it works."

Bets handed the cord to her, and the bestselling author plugged in her dying computer. The symbol showed charging, and a "Woohoo" slipped out of Betsy as well as an "I'm going to strangle my best friend."

"What and to whom are you doing this?"

Dillon's question remained unanswered when Betsy spotted Andrew and Rosie. They walked into the room – together. She remained calm but reflected on why she hadn't stayed in bed under the covers that morning. *Father, what is my friend up to now?*

CHAPTER TWO

"Betsy Stevenson, you slipped out of the room faster than a rabbit eluding a fox. I thought we'd have breakfast together at least, but then I ran into Mr. Pickle in the lobby. He's invited me to listen in on the class Dillon McCloud is—Lord, in Heaven – it's you."

"If you mean Dillon McCloud, then yes, it is. And who are you?"

"I'm Rose Wilford. You can call me Rosie. Betsy is my friend. We go way back. And, please stop me. I'm babbling."

Bets braced herself, thinking Rose would tackle Dillon in one of her customary hugs. But all wonders of wonders, her usually boisterous friend stayed in her spot and gawked at the famous author.

"If you're a friend of Betsy, you're one of mine too. It *was* unfortunate she and I couldn't spend more time together yesterday evening." Dillon winked at Betsy, then proceeded to hug Rose.

Betsy laughed out loud when Dillon shut down Rose's ability to speak. And her chubby face showed utter disbelief. Betsy loved it and said, "Her husband has searched for a way to silence her for years. Took one statement from you to do it." Betsy wiped at her wet cheeks.

"You're not one bit funny, Bets. And, we'll talk later about how and why you neglected to mention you hung out with Dillon." Rose's reclaimed voice rose with each word. At the end, a snort slipped out.

"Ladies, I'll leave you in Ms. McCloud's capable hands. Have fun in class." Then Andrew added, "She'll have tons of helpful information to share with you."

"I do." Dillon straightened the folder next to Betsy's computer. "And I'm glad you're not stealing her away from me like you did last night."

The man's shoulders stiffened. "That's not altogether true. And you know it. Will you excuse me? I see another of my clients."

Betsy realized in less than a dozen words that these two knew each other, and Dillon's expression screamed that she wanted to follow him, with fists flying. Bets stepped in. "Did you see the decorations Amy brought for our table?"

Dillon removed her gaze from Betsy's editor and looked at her. "Yes, I did. The center décor stood out. Did you have to reinforce the table to hold it?"

"I'm sorry I missed it," Rosie chimed in.

"Rose, it's obvious you're still miffed, for whatever reason. How about we ask Dillon if we can sit with her at lunch? I'll guarantee you've already talked to the conference organizers and have a meal plan in place. Am I right?" Betsy read her bestie like a book.

"Lunch sounds wonderful, but don't be so quick to assume I'd go so far as to finagle anything of the sort."

"I ask again. Am I right?"

"I gave them my credit card last night for everything. And I can't wait to hear Dillon's talk. But hey, Bets, you never know – I might even learn a thing or two to help you with your writing."

~~~

Not that Betsy wrote mystery novels, but with the information Dillon shared and the notes she gave the class – she considered changing genres. Conflict. Suspense. Secrets. Those three components played an essential role in those kinds of stories.

And all three had shown up with Dillon and Andrew's strange interaction earlier, which intrigued Betsy. And the reaction the famed author gave her editor – they had a history. *So after we eat, I'll talk to Rose about my suspicions. She'll find out what's going on.*

Speaking of lunch, Betsy spied Dillon's table across the room and headed to it. When they were a short distance away, she said, "Rosie, sitting with her does not give you the right to do all the talking. She allows us to ask her writing questions. To pick her brain."

"Oh, I'm going to do more than pick her brain, Bets. I'm going to harvest the whole crop. Wonder if your editor and her—"

"Hush on all accounts, Rose. We're within earshot of her table."

"And quit pinching me. I'm an adult and don't require supervision."

"There are days I'm not so sure. I'll use a phrase our teacher used this morning. 'Your character has to be entertaining and perplexing all at the same time.' Rosebud, that was the best description of you I had ever heard. Now sit down."

"You're talking descriptions without me?" Dillon

unfolded her napkin and placed it on her lap. "I love talking about this topic more than any other. While I'm reading, descriptors make me turn the page. Don't elaborate on a bush and its blooms. Instead, tell me about the character's quirks."

"May I join you?"

"Sure, Mr. Pickle, pull up a chair next to me. We were talking about des…descry…"

"Rose, please call me Andrew. And they are descriptors. Dillon, what other techniques can mystery writers use to further their plots?"

She delayed answering him, and Betsy swore she heard her whisper the word, "Ignoramus." *Lord, we have a problem here, and I feel like I'm in the middle of whatever is going on with these tw—*

"Dillon, I don't mean to interrupt your thought process, but…" Rosie took a roll from the basket in front of her and buttered it. "But you are adorable to watch when your brain is a-churning. Isn't she, Bets?"

Betsy called Heaven her forever home and prayed she'd reach it at that moment. And she hoped upon hope that Rose would stuff the flaky biscuit into her mouth to quiet any more comments.

The mystery writer cleared her throat. "To answer Andrew's question—you can use any component from a mystery in all the other genres. But in the Christian market, the publishers prefer the *murder* happens off-camera."

Did Dillon accentuate the 'M' word and give the editor a sideward glance? Betsy studied Andrew, and he paid no attention to the author's comment and continued to eat the salad the staff delivered to their table.

"And the crime scene cannot be too gruesome. A

good example is with Betsy's book. She writes romantic comedy. She's not going to have a dead person hanging from a chandelier in the middle of a writer's—"

Dillon stopped, and her eyes widened. A slight pinkish color on her cheeks also surfaced. Betsy considered calling for help, but her new friend finally said, "I'm fine. However, I inadvertently divulged one of the crimes in my next book."

I do believe with the reaction you gave, Ms. Bestselling Author, you just lied. Yes, Rosie, we have a mystery brewing in front of us.

~~~

And the plot thickened when the main course arrived. The mystery writer dove into hers as if no one else sat at her table. Bets nibbled on rice and considered a couple of conversation starters, but then Dillon said, "I know Betsy writes, but what else do you two do?"

"They're full-time RVers," Andrew interjected. "With Betsy being mobile, it makes book signings a breeze."

"They are full-time what?"

"What Andrew is trying to say is we travel around in our RV for six months. The rest of the time, we're in Florida, soaking up the sun, and working at Rose's second-hand store." Betsy speared a piece of chicken and stuck it in her mouth but regretted it when Dillon grabbed her arm.

"You *both* have recreational vehicles? WOW!!! I've dreamt of traveling around the country in one of them. The open road. Story ideas from people I'd meet along the way. A new campground to set up in every night."

"Hold onto your hat, Dillon. This segues into a great idea Betsy has for a writing contest. The best essay an author sends in will win a ride-along in her RV—anywhere they want to go. Her friends on Facebook tell her all the time they'd enjoy tagging along on a trip with them."

"Dillon and Andrew aren't interested in my off-the-wall notions, Rosebud. Let's return to the subject of—"

"Of RVing, Betsy! Your idea is brilliant. And I have another one. If Dillon agrees, we can take off in my Minnie Winnie on Monday morning and travel anywhere we want to go." Rose took off on a rendition of Willie Nelson's famous song.

"Dear friend of mine, there are two important parts of this equation you're forgetting: the first is whether Dillon would drop everything to come along with us, and the second is our husbands. We'd have to tell them we've made alternate plans and are not coming home. And right now, my hubby is here in a campground, waiting for me."

"He's not alone! I thought of everything and dropped Larry off at your trailer on my way here in the teeny-tiniest chance we'd follow this weekend with an adventure of our own. So what do you think, Dillon? Are you up for this crazy plan? And Betsy, how about you?"

Excitement and trepidation filled Betsy at the thought of the famous author traveling with them. "Rose, I'm game *if* our husbands, and Dillon, agree."

"They will. And, as usual, our travels have to include stops at Taco Bell. Oh, I have to share a saying I saw on Facebook yesterday. 'A taco is a beef love letter in a corn envelope you mail to your stomach.'"

The one-liner must have awakened Andrew. He sputtered, spit, and held his midsection as if he'd lose his liver if he didn't. When he managed to talk again, he said, "That's too funny. I have a friend at Taco Bell's corporate office. I'll suggest they use this for their slogan."

"And, we can't forget S'mores. If those two things don't entice you, nothing will. So Dillon, are you ready to experience tons of fun?"

"I am! And I'm not even going to check my schedule. I'll tell Arlene we're going where the RV takes us. By the way, where do we want to go?" Dillon rose from her seat and pranced around the table.

"Praise the Lord and pass the turtle soup."

Andrew shot a look at Rose and then to the soup sitting in front of him. The man seemed to contemplate what he'd eaten and when he swallowed the bite he'd taken, he said, "I've never tasted turtle soup, but if this is what it tastes like, it's pretty good."

Betsy wanted to inform her editor he had consumed tomato bisque soup, but before she could, he announced, "Ladies, your RV adventure sounds interesting, but I have to go check on Amy. She informed me earlier she planned to work through lunch." Andrew placed his napkin on the table and left.

Again, Dillon's gaze appeared to follow him out of the room. But this time, she giggled. She eventually regained her ability to speak, and what Betsy heard shocked her. "I'm not surprised the man still doesn't cook, or he'd know the difference between turtle and tomato."

Turtle soup is one of Rosie's sayings – not a type of soup, in this case. And why is Dillon using the word "still?"

~~~

"You are going where?"

IT'S A MYSTERY...BIRDS

"Ben, we're heading to St. Augustine first, but our final destination will be Asheville, North Carolina. Our new friend has never been RVing. So we've voted, and it's a put-it-in-gear-and-go event."

Dead silence on the other end of the phone told Betsy her husband had either passed out or spent the time figuring out his rebuttal. She held her breath and waited for the reasons as to why they needed to come home. "When Rosie dropped Larry at our rig the other night, we figured you'd call with a grandiose plan to continue your travels. I'm glad I have you on speaker. Lar's head nodding reminds me of a bobblehead. Seriously, Bets, this sounds like a fun trip for you two to get to know your favorite writer."

Betsy removed the phone from her ear and bopped the side of her head. *It has to be wax in there, blocking my ability to hear. No way my hubby is okay with this without a discussion.* "Ben, can you repeat yourself? I don't think I heard you. Larry, talk to me."

"He's fine, Betsy. You go with our blessing."

"Are yo—"

"Are you wondering why we're so agreeable? Larry said Rose drove them to Daytona, and she kept her cool all the way. Our Rosie is growing up."

"She and I are ready to leave the nest, but we'll return, and I'll have another book on its way to completion."

"Seriously, you two can tackle whatever comes your way. And you have the roadside assistance card. Call them if you run into anything."

"No worries, Ben. Our Heavenly Father is riding along and will take good care of us. And while I have my phone in my hand, I have to email Mom and let her know about our travels. Of course, they won't be as exotic as the world cruise she's on, but we're excited."

"Talk to you soon."

Betsy clicked off her phone. *What are we doing?*

~~~

Monday morning dawned, and Betsy made her way to the hotel lobby to check out. As she waited in line, the praise and worship music from the night before kept her company. She hummed *Amazing Grace.*

She returned the keys and strolled to the coffee shop. Delicious aromas filled the air. Betsy poured a cup, but when Amy walked up with disheveled hair, she handed it to her. "You look like you need this more than I do. Did you get any sleep, or did you write all night?"

"Both. Sort of." Amy yawned. "I don't get a chance to write nonstop very often, so I took full advantage of it. I'm glad we spent time together the first night. I enjoyed hearing about your journey. Now, I can't wait to get home and review what I've written and the class notes."

"I'll look at them while we're traveling. And maybe get some writing done too."

"Oh, I almost forgot. Here are your books." Amy retrieved them from her bag and gave them to Betsy.

"Don't know how I spaced those out. Guess I'm excited about our upcoming trip. Thanks!" Betsy stashed her books in her luggage then grabbed a business card, handing it to her friend. "Email me your phone number, and we'll be in touch when we get to Fort Myers.".

"I will, and if this trip with your favorite author goes well, put me on the list to join you on your next girl's/writer's adventure." Amy blushed.

"You are next, my dear. Rosie and I will soon be

known as chauffeurs to famous and budding novelists."

"After Ms. McCloud disclosed she was hitching a ride with you two, you'll have tons of requests from other authors."

"You're probably right. When it's your turn to ride along, you're responsible for the decorations." Betsy hugged her new friend. "Blessings on your writing, Amy. Can't wait to read your book."

"Enjoy, and it's time for me to catch a bus."

They strolled out of the hotel, and the young woman rushed to a waiting bus to the airport. She turned and waved. "I'll talk to you soon."

"Look forward to it." Betsy walked a short distance and joined her traveling companions out in the parking lot. Their bags surrounded them outside instead of where they belonged – inside the RV. She asked the stupidest question, "What's wrong?"

"We've run into a snag." Sweat dripped down Rosie's chin. "All of this is NOT going into my RV. Our only solution is to rent a U-Haul, or you could catch Ben and Larry before they get too far. They can help us out of this dilemma."

"I'm on it." She clicked on Ben's number, and when he answered, she said, "My dearest hubby, you and Larry have to take a side trip. Bags aren't fitting inside. And the September heat, radiating from the pavement, is irritating me."

"It is a scorcher, and we're glad you called. You may have noticed that we forgot to say our goodbyes last night when we talked."

"Oops! We did space that part out." Betsy pulled the phone from her mouth and yelled. "Rosebud, we're in hot molasses, but there's a bright spot. If *you* didn't have these extra bags, we'd have forgotten to call our hubbies."

"I'll give Lar an extra squeeze when I see him, but speak for yourself, Missy – you told me you had one shirt left after you dribbled on the other one. Now I end up wheeling a suitcase the size of the space shuttle behind me to our new home. Is Andrew Pickle hiding in there?"

"I hope not."

Dillon's comment made Betsy laugh when she envisioned him inside her suitcase, but on the other hand, she wondered about her sassy retort.

"Bets, are you still with me?"

She let Dillon's remark go and said, "Ben, I'm here, but our friend wants an inventory of what's in my bag. Rosie, all I have are the clothes I packed and the books I purchased." She then turned her attention back to her hubby. "You and Larry have to help us."

"We're on our way. Oh, and before I forget – Lar and I are staying here for an extra day or two. The roof on Sassy Seconds *Two* will still be there when we get home. Douglas said it's close to completion. Did I tell you the campground has a hot tub and—"

"When I see your smiling faces, you can fill me in on all the extra amenities at your RV Park. Talk to you soon." Betsy hung up and deposited her phone in the back pocket of her jean capris.

~~~

While they waited for Ben and Larry, the ladies took turns unloading the contents of their suitcases into the RV. When Betsy finished, she brought her bag outside. She turned to her friends, "Our flying-by-the-seat-of-our-pants thinking didn't work so well this time. Hope it improves."

"It will, and it's why I adore you, Mrs. Elizabeth Stevenson." Ben hugged Betsy from behind.

"Who are you, and why do you have your hands on me." Bets gave her husband a big smacker. "You are my knight in blue-jean shorts and a t-shirt who saves me from whatever calamity I create.

"And it won't cost you anything for transporting your goods."

"Don't count on it. This will cost both of you." Larry saddled next to Rose and bumped her.

"You, old poop, don't start acting up. You're in the presence of a famous person. Dillon McCloud, I'd like you to meet my husband, Larry. The man standing next to Betsy is Ben, her hubby. They're harmless but ornery."

"It's a pleasure to meet you. The ladies have talked nonstop about you and your adventures."

"I hope she's zipped it about my close calls in our RV. Winnie B here hasn't seen any mishaps, so Rose, let's keep it that way. I also brought a dozen grocery bags. I'll leave them with you to store your belongings." Larry held a Sharpie®. "You can mark what's in them."

"I'll take three bags and a pen." Dillon took them and disappeared into the RV. A second later, she leaned out, "Ben and Larry, can I ask you a big favor?"

"What do you need?" Ben smiled as he picked up one of the suitcases.

"Since none of us thought about me not going to Fort Myers after the end of our travels, I need you to ship my luggage to my agent? She's always home. I'll write down Arlene's address."

"Way to go, Dillon. You solved a mystery we didn't even know we had. And I'll answer for Ben. His favorite thing to do is go to the post office."

"It is? And I will."

"Now that we've figured out who's doing what, I'll take the rest of the shopping bags. But first..." Rosie gave her husband a hug and a smooch he'd talk about on their way home. And when she let him go, she said, "Lar, please don't worry about Winnie B. I'll take care of her."

"Bets, I'll take one of those kisses." Ben puckered his lips.

She happily indulged his request. "I love you too, Benjamin. Now it's Matilda's turn." Their pooch scampered to the open window, and Bets snuggled with her. "I'm going to miss you and your dad. Tell him to take you on lots of walks."

"She'll remind me." Ben returned to the truck, and Betsy tagged along. He opened the back door.

"Since those two stole all the grocery bags, what did you bring me to put my clothes in?"

"I brought you a box for what you don't hang up. It'll fit at the end of whichever bed you sleep in."

"What a guy."

"Tell her what else you did."

Betsy's curiosity piqued. *Did he buy me a present? No, not enough time in between her call and them driving to meet them.* "What's behind your back?"

"I mapped out all the Taco Bells from Daytona to Asheville. Key in the address, and P.I.T.S. will take you right to it."

"That's sweet of you, but don't count on Pain In The Shorts. She has trouble getting us anywhere the first time around." Betsy chuckled at the name they'd given their GPS.

"Lar, here is my suitcase – filled to overflowing."

Rose exited the RV. "There isn't room for a sock in there. The campgrounds have laundries, but we'll be too busy kicking the light fantastic to do—"

"It's 'tripping the light fantastic.'"

"Whatever, I tend to trip when I'm walking. And who wants to do chores when we're on the way to walk on the Appalachian Trail. Note to all: I don't hike. My gift is praising the Lord and snorting."

"Goodbye, my crazy Rose. Keep us in the loop."

Larry kissed Rose, which stopped any further communication from her. Betsy elected to egg them on. "Lar, when you two get finished, I want you to know I'll watch your wife like a hawk. She's not allowed to go out alone, but I'll bet she'll find ways to help humanity."

"Without us? Tell me it isn't true?" Ben swept Betsy into his arms and kissed her too.

After she came up for air, Bets said, "That'll hold me for a day or two. And we'll call you for assistance, like this morning, if we run into trouble. We'll be fine, but keep us in your prayers. Now we're off."

CHAPTER THREE

Rose took the driver's seat, and as she shifted Winnie B into drive, she prayed her usual way—OUT LOUD. No doubt Heaven woke to her requests for their safety and for them to have adventures galore. "And amen. We are on the—"

"Road again, and I'm ready, Mrs. Wilford...almost" Betsy buckled herself in the passenger's seat and searched for Restorative Campground and Cabins in St. Augustine, Florida. "Hold on, Rosie, I'm having trouble. Their website isn't workin—"

"Dillon, since you're much younger than us, you're more tech-savvy. Can you come here and get her phone?"

"No." Bets fiddled for another second, and the directions showed on the screen. "I have it." Betsy placed her phone in the holder, and it spoke, "In four hundred feet head north. Head north in four hundred feet."

"It's nagging when you repeat yourself, P.I.T.S." Rose announced. "Watch me now. I'm proceeding four hundred feet and am going to head north."

"While Bets was locating their directions, I've been on an online chat with them. They are a full-service campground." Dillon paused, then added, "Is there anything you want me to ask them?"

Betsy twisted around in her seat. "Ask if they have an early check-in charge?" Her experience in this matter raised a red flag and prompted her to question the park's policy.

"She said if the spot is empty, we're able to check-in anytime we want."

"As I said a moment ago, we're on the road again." Rose hummed the song as she pulled the Minnie Winnie forward.

"Yes, and how about we hush so our new friend can write?" Betsy peered over her left shoulder at Dillon, who sat in front of her opened laptop.

"Rosie, I'm buckled in. But don't hit the highway quite yet. Do you have a strap to hold my computer in place? Hey, chewing gum would work." Dillon laughed.

"I have the solution, but at this rate, we won't make St. Augustine until next Thursday." Rosie stopped and hurried to the kitchen. She opened a drawer and removed a packet. "Larry and Ben swear by this stuff. It should work 'cause Lar said astronauts use it at the Space Station."

"Good to know." Dillon took a small gob of the goop in her hand.

Rose returned to the driver's seat. "Since we're in our respective spots, may I proceed to said route?"

"Hold on again." Betsy halted their forward motion while watching Dillon roll the putty-looking matter between her thumb and index finger. The author then placed each wad she'd made under the corners of her laptop.

"We're good to go." Dillon wiggled her computer. "It's not going anywhere."

Rosie accelerated, and within minutes, Winnie B merged onto I-95. Betsy peeked at her friend. The driving lessons she'd taken taught her how to drive, but they also gave her a calmness behind the wheel. And as the traffic came to a dead stop ahead, Bets prayed Rose's composure stayed put.

Incoherent sounds reverberated from the driver's side, which communicated to Betsy as prayers, and she united with her friend's petitions as traffic crawled. Ten straight minutes they traveled at a snail's pace.

Then like magic, the highway cleared, and everyone sped away to their final destinations. Rose included. Betsy checked the side of the freeway, but no wreck, stalled vehicle, or police cars gave them a clue as to what caused the snarl.

About the time a mileage sign caught Betsy's attention, Dillon said, "We will reach our destination in a total of fifty-two miles?"

Rose pointed at the phone. "Shorter days are my favorite. It gets us into the spot early, where we can relax. So, how are you enjoying your first RV adventure?"

"We've only gone a few miles, but I'm already sold. This is the life. Everything is within arms-length, the bathroom is steps away, and the ability to make a sandwich whenever I get hungry is a huge perk. Fabulous. I haven't even touched on what we'll see on our way to wherever."

"If you ever get in the driver's seat, you can't fix lunch."

"Good point, Rose."

"And another excellent point – I see a semi-truck slowing down in front of us. Rosie?" Betsy pressed her foot on the imaginary brake pedal, and white knuckles held the door with a death grip until her friend brought the rig to a complete stop.

"Dillon, this is the part of traveling in an RV that will put wrinkles where they don't belong. And Betsy's overreaction – we'll talk about later. How does Ben do it?"

Traffic started to move again. "My hubby does fine. And if Larry witnessed your last bit of expertise at stopping on a dime, he'd give you an A+."

"And since you're my bestie, he doesn't have to be privy to me maneuvering Winnie B sideways to get it accomplished."

"You two are a blast to travel with. Are we there yet?"

"Less than thirty miles."

After Rose's ETA, chatter stalled. Betsy took out her notebook and made notes concerning her next novel. Every so often, she'd glance up at the road because she didn't want to miss the Welcome to St. Augustine sign.

And when she spotted it, Bets laid her notebook and pen down and whipped out her phone to take pictures of it. She also noticed GPS led them through the busiest part of town on their way to their campground.

Mumbling began to her left, and the words Betsy intended to stay in her head tumbled out, "Sister, you've navigated I-95 – what has your undies in a knot at a busy traffic light?"

"For your information, my underwear is riding in its proper place. But, oh my goodness, check this out. According to P.I.T.S., we're two-tenths of a mile from our destination. Ladies, this means we're across the street from the Atlantic Ocean. Thank You, Lord."

All heads rotated to the right, about the time a honk sounded behind them. "Rosie, the light is green. Get this thing parked, so we can explore these cute shops and find a bite to eat. I'm famished."

Rose pulled away, and in seconds the RV sat idling outside the office at Restorative Campground and Cabins. Betsy reached for the door handle, but two men in blue shirts halted her exit.

"Good afternoon. What name is your reservation under?"

"Betsy Stevenson."

"Not any longer, it's not. I'm picking up the tab on our travels." Dillon opened the side door and stepped out. "The reservation is now under Dillon McCloud."

The attendant radioed in the change, but the walkie-talkie squawked when he released his finger from the button. The sound subsided, and a woman on the other end asked, "Paul, can you repeat the name you gave me? A famous author wouldn't stay…"

Dillon stole the two-way radio from the man and spoke into it. "The 'famous' author wants to stay here. If you'd like, I can come to the office and prove I'm her. I'll even sign a book for you." The mystery writer leaned into the RV. "Rose and Bets, come out here. This is fun."

They did and positioned themselves behind the writer. A second later, a robust lady rambled down the stairs and headed in their direction. Pure joy etched on her face. It announced to the world, "This is a celebrity, and we'll be giving her the royal treatment."

"Ms. McCloud, welcome! We have the ideal spot for your RV. What is it you're driving?"

"My driver, Rose Wilford, will help you with that

information. I don't have a clue what we're in, but..."

Dillon stopped talking, and Bets assumed it had to do with the statement she'd made. And Rosie's scowl verified she'd found no humor in being called a 'driver.' Bets whispered to her, "She was joking. Dillon had a live one and milked it for all it was worth."

"Oh, she did now?"

"Absolutely. That woman who works here is so enamored with Dillon, we could park in the highest-priced pull-through site, and they'd not know it until Security verified who occupied the spot."

"Let's do it."

"Rosie, if I didn't know better, I'd think you're losing it. Can't you tell when I'm kidding?" Betsy hugged her friend. "Envision it. When I hit the big time, I'll have you as *my* 'driver' on those occasions we take off by ourselves."

"And all the hugs you'll ever want. By the way, I get the charade now. Betsy, you're such a smoozer. And our author friend is going to find out she's..."

"What *is* she going to find out, Rosie?"

A sudden gust of wind halted conversation, and they dashed to their home on wheels to stay dry. Raindrops the size of quarters splattered the windshield and pitter-pattered on the roof of Winnie B.

Rose's smug expression reminded Betsy how much her friend hated water. Especially after the last tropical storm. Bets loved rain but thanked the Lord for them not getting stuck on the highway in the torrential downpour.

The storm moved on, but in its wake – it left palm fronds scattered about on the streets. A two-man crew, working next to the office, hooked a trailer to a golf cart and picked up the piles of debris.

"I've just arrived, and I'm impressed with two things," Dillon broke the silence inside the RV.

"And they are?"

"How efficient they are here and how strong this putty is. My computer won't budge."

Betsy laughed at the author's struggles to remove her laptop. "Guess we're eating all of our meals out. The table is officially Dillon's workspace for the entire trip. I'm still starving. Can we go eat?"

"Can I free her laptop from bondage first?" Rosie seized it, and it yielded. "You have to know what you're doing."

"Thank you, and I was kidding. You're no more my 'driver' than Porky Pig is my nephew. And, if you ever let me take the wheel, you can tell people I'm chauffeuring you around the country. That'll get their attention."

"Dillon, you're going to fit in with the Early Birds. I'll explain the name later. And about…" Rose hesitated.

"Go ahead, tell Dillon what you thought."

"I hate to admit this, and I'm embarrassed, but I thought you were flaunting your fame earlier. But Betsy rectified the situation. Will you accept my apology?"

"Of course. Oh, and about me having an uppity attitude, Bets and my trip in the elevator the other day explained it doesn't exist. And I'm thrilled you two let me tag along. We're going to *Always Enjoy the Journey*, as Betsy's book confirms."

"Quit with the compliments. Betsy's head is big enough already." Rose nestled next to Dillon at the banquette. "With her multiple book signings, having a famous author befriend her, and now you're traveling together. Next thing, she'll be asking me to do her laundry."

"Thanks for the reminder. After we eat, wherever you choose, I have to throw in a load. Please don't let me forget."

~~~

After dinner and shopping, washing clothes became a distant second to crafting the perfect S'more, but a problem arose. They'd reached the bottom of the marshmallow bag. Betsy jumped up. "I'll fetch the new bag, and I better call Ben to fill him in on our first day."

"Tell Lar I'll talk to him later and to give Baby a hug for me."

While she chatted with her hubby, Betsy viewed a person out of the window. The stocky-built man wore dark slacks and a polo shirt, plus a safari hat, which wasn't a typical outfit you wore camping. As he strode past the RV, he turned away.

"Ben, excuse me for interrupting, but right now, my hebbie-jeebies are on high alert," Betsy explained what she'd seen.

"Your writer brain is working overtime."

Betsy played with the pen in the cupholder. "You're probably right. Talk to you later. The girls are waiting for me. Relay that Rosie will call Larry later."

As she approached her friends, Bets let go of the lingering uneasiness and snatched the marshmallows off the picnic table. As she neared the circle of chairs, she overheard the last of Dillon's words. "Rosie, I can't call my boyfriend."

Huh? Dillon has a special someone? Betsy's head filled with more questions than answers, and she forgot she held the bag of marshmallows – which were now smushed. She struggled to refluff them, but to no avail.

"This whole thing is turning into a mystery."

"And while Betsy is talking to herself and demolishing our dessert, I'll ask you to expound on where your beau is?" Rose stuck the metal hanger with two extra-large, redesigned marshmallows into the roaring fire. They soon burst into flames.

"Rosie, if it interests you, you might pay attention to the near-burning embers at the end of your stick." Betsy hit her hanger against her friend's, and the charred remains fell into the fire. "See, they're toast."

"I prefer to call them crispy."

"Try again, and this time watch them, so they're edible." Betsy shifted her seat closer to her friend. "Here, let me help you."

Rose pulled her sleeve from Betsy's grasp. "Get away from me and let Dillon answer my question about the locale of her boyfriend."

"Thomas is a journalist. Right now, he's in Australia. I don't know much else. He'll text me on a secure phone."

"Do you have to kill us now that you've divulged this information?" Rose's mouth dropped open.

"I'll have to consider it if you listen in on our conversations." Dillon snickered. "I'm kidding. I can tell you our relationship is a tad different than most. We've been dating on and off nine years, and we've spent one year together in the same city. The rest is a week here or there."

"Gives you plenty of time to write." Betsy thought of her desk and Ben being around all the time. "Sorry, that came out wrong."

"Not at all. I have plenty of time to write. However, there are days it takes a multitude of angels to carry me to my desk chair to get another page written."

"If you're a dawdler, *like me,* how do you write two books in a year?" Betsy laid her skewer down and gave her full attention to Dillon.

"When I come up with an idea for a book, I do an extensive synopsis. Sometimes up to five or six pages. And I write the end first. Then I go back and fill in the dialogue between characters, conflicts and solve the mystery. And I write The End!"

"Dillon, there's more I want to ask you about writing, but your laundry is waiting for you." Betsy folded up her lawn chair. "Come on, Rose, wake up."

"Instead of laundry, I'm going in to write." Dillon doused the flames and placed the screen on the fire pit. "It's interesting when I talk about the craft of writing. It helps me work through writer's block. Laundry can wait until tomorrow morning."

The author's words struck a chord with Betsy as she put the chairs away. *I'm not alone. She deals with procrastination too. Thank You, Lord. And later, when I go to bed, I'll see if Dillon's method of writing works.* "It's worth a try."

"Are you coming tonight?" Rosie held the door open."

"I'm on my way."

Once inside, they discussed who ranked highest in using the bathroom first. Betsy suggested, "Rosie, it will be our esteemed guest. Even if your bladder is older than the rest of ours."

"By a few months. And I agree. Ms. McCloud, you go ahead." Rose gave Bets a sideways glance and added. "I've made an executive decision, which overrides yours. It's my RV, and I'm next after Dillon."

While Betsy waited for the bathroom line to clear, she

grabbed her computer and climbed to the bed above the cab of the truck. Her home away from home. The shortened height made slouching more of an option than sitting up straight.

Multiple trips up and down the ladder to her new "bedroom" tickled Betsy. *Doesn't this classify as exercise – my heart is pounding?* She settled in with her computer on her lap. A peek at the couch showed Rosie reading a magazine.

A constant pecking noise from the rear bed echoed in the small area. Betsy imagined Dillon's fingers as they flew across her keyboard, creating another book for her adoring fans. *Me included. What will it be about? Is there really someone hanging from a ceiling fan in it?*

"Ladies?"

Bets nearly tossed her computer to the floor below when Dillon shouted the one word but caught it in mid-flight. "I'm awake."

"Wanted to tell you, I've set my phone for 5:00. Tomorrow morning, I'll slip out and take my shower while my laundry is on the wash cycle." Dillon yawned.

"Don't buy quarters." Rose dropped her magazine and opened a drawer next to her. "Take as many as you need."

"I have plenty. Florence, the camp host, handed me three rolls of quarters for all of us to use. Bets, I hope you brought some of your books. She wants copies of all of them to put in the office. We can take them in the morning."

"Then, after laundry." Rosie reclaimed the magazine off the couch. "We have to stroll around the city one last time to see the old estates with their stately oaks. It says here, 'Spanish moss isn't a moss but a bromeliad – a perennial herb in the pineapple family.'"

"You're a bevy of information at 10:30 p.m. You go ahead and do more research. I am going to bed." Betsy closed her computer and laid it at the foot of the bed. She curled up under the covers and waited for blissful sleep.

"This is the textbook place to commit a murder," The mystery writer's voice rang out in the darkness again.

"What?" Betsy asked but then wondered if she'd dreamed someone spoke. "Hello, did either of you say something?"

"It was me. Rosie's comment reminded me of research I did years ago. It's the oldest city in America. Plus, some of the buildings are haunted." A light switched on. "And we can't forget the Fountain of Youth. St. Augustine is a town full of mystery and intrigue."

"What you're saying, Dillon, that this is the ideal place to whack someone off."

"Rosie, you've been watching way too many episodes of Dateline and 48 Hours."

"They're interesting, Bets, but you're probably right. Let's discuss this topic at breakfast. I'm tired. Sweet Dreams."

Yea, right. I'm going to sleep now after talking about haunted buildings. It's not happening.

~~~

Betsy startled awake, but silence filled the RV. "Great, now I'm never going to get back to sleep after discuss—" Just then, another scream pierced the quiet. Her bare feet hit the floor without touching the ladder. "Rosie, something is going on out there."

"You think?"

"No time for sass. Where's Dillon? We have to find

her."

They slid on their slippers and hurried to the commotion outside. Dillon stood in the middle of the crowd that had gathered, and she pointed in two different directions at the same time. Her sobs made her words unrecognizable.

A police car arrived, and a man exited the vehicle. "Hello, I'm Detective Dennis Wilds. Dispatch said a person saw a dead body here in the park."

"Sir, I'm Dillon McCloud. The person was lying in the laundry room. I don't know if he's dead or unconscious."

"Please go to the office and wait for me. I'm going to check out the crime scene. Everyone else, the laundry room is closed until further notice. Do not leave the campground. I will be talking to you later."

"Can my friends come along?" Dillon gestured to the crowd. "They're out there somewhere."

"I'll allow them to go with you, but don't touch anything. The crime could have started anywhere on the property."

Betsy corralled both of her friends and marched them into the office. And one gander at the famous author told her that Dillon needed to take a seat, or she'd faint dead away.

"Hold onto her, Rose."

Betsy located a row of chairs at the back of the room and directed Dillon to sit in one of them.

"Please, tell me I'm asleep, and this is a bad dream."

"It isn't, but I suspect the detective will come back in a short while to get your statement. However, I'm not sure you're in any shape to give an account." Rosie brought one of the chairs and sat it next to Dillon. "Dear, whatever it is that happened, we're here for you."

Betsy quit listening and scanned the area outside the window. Other campers milled around as if they attended an early-morning coffee club. *People, don't you know there's a possible crime scene under your feet. Wake up.*

A door slammed, cutting off Betsy's nattering to herself, and she focused on the detective as he entered the side door of the office.

"Ms. McCloud, you told me a few minutes ago you were washing clothes. Is that right? And you saw a person lying on the floor."

"Yes."

"There isn't a body in the laundry room. However, the cleaning lady was there, mopping the floor. She said she arrived at 3:00 this morning, and nothing appeared out of the ordinary throughout her shift."

Dillon darted out of the room and across the rocked driveway. Betsy and Rose rushed behind her. Yellow tape stopped them from entering the room, but Betsy snuck a peek. The officer had taped across the first washing machine.

The cleaning woman came into view, and the detective asked her, "Are there security cameras in here?"

"They've not installed them. The office is the only place."

"Thank you for your time. Don't go anywhere. I may have more questions." The detective faced Dillon. "Let's go to the office so I can get your statement."

~~~

"Ms. McCloud, take your time. Tell me everything you saw." Detective Wilds placed his pen on the pad of paper he held.

"As I said, I planned to do my laundry. With my first load in, I left to take my shower. When I came out – that's when I saw someone lying on the floor, between the washers and dryers. Officer, I write about stuff like this but never expected I'd witness a crime."

"What did he have on?"

"I don't know if they were male or female, but the person wore a baggy Hawaiian shirt and tan shorts. They came to their knees." Color rose on Dillon's cheeks. "I write mysteries, but the items on or around him or her you don't usually find at a crime scene."

"What were they?"

"They wore a pair of frilly underwear on their head, making it impossible to recognize who they were. They also had a ukulele lying on their chest. Like they were playing it as they died." Tears erupted again. "I had nothing to do with this, Off—"

"Ms. McCloud, I'll ask other residents if they saw a suspicious person wearing the clothing you described. Personally, since there isn't a body, I'm leaning on the theory a prankster is on the loose."

"If it's a prank, I'm not finding it funny. Not one bit." Dillon turned but must have changed her mind. "I guess I better extend our stay. We're not going anywhere. Whoever did this is not going to get away with this. They scared ten years off my life." She rushed to the counter.

"Detective, this probably isn't worth mentioning, but I saw a man walking around last night. Long pants aren't what a typical camper wears."

"Go on."

"But his clothing doesn't fit the description Dillon gave you." Betsy rubbed her forehead. "Now that air has hit my words, they sound lame."

"Nothing is insignificant. If you see the man again – pay closer attention to him." He put his pad of paper away. "When Ms. McCloud is done, tell her I'll be in touch with her later today." The detective exited out the side door.

"Betsy, we have to plot out our next move, so it's a good idea to remain on scene."

"Police jargon coming out of you leans toward ridiculous, Rosie, but this is no laughing matter. There's a possible nut case on the loose around here. While we wait for Dillon, I'm going to look around."

Betsy walked by the library in the far corner of the office and spied a book titled, *To Catch a Thief.* Laughter engulfed her at the image of Rose chasing down a criminal with her stumpy legs. No chance she'd outrun the hoodlum.

"I don't know where your mind is, Betsy Stevenson, and why you're chuckling. I wish I had the ability to entertain myself as you do. Anyway, Dillon's busy making reservations for who knows how long, and I'm left alone to solve this mystery."

"Rosie, I'm not counting on you to solve anything. You can't figure out a crossword puzzle. How do you plan on finding a person who has faded into thin air? He's crazy if he's roaming around in the same clothes. I'm going with it being a hoax, and the person is halfway to Savannah by now."

"But what if the criminal *is* here and *is* lurking around in the same clothes? We're wasting valuable time here instead of looking for the would-be felon."

"We'll have plenty of time to search, Rose." Dillon walked up, holding a receipt. "We're good for another week. Florence is so accommodating. It's like they knew we'd need to stay longer."

"Now it's time to hunker down in the RV and discuss the details of the crime." Rose opened the office door. "So far, Bets has not been much assistance. Come on, you two. We have work to do."

"There's not much to discuss, but I have an idea. I'll formulate it while we walk to the camper."

Betsy followed her comrades across the campground and speculated on different scenarios that might be going on in Dillon's mind. After what she'd encountered that morning, Bets had no clue what she'd reveal to them.

They reached the door, and Dillon said as they entered the RV. "I'm going to do a vlog to let my fans in on what's going on. So they can pray." She turned and began to fiddle with her phone.

"Is that a good idea with it being an open case? Detective Wilds won't like this." *Lord, I know at any minute her forensic training is going to kick in. And then she will put her phone away.*

"Hi everyone. I've had an exciting morning. Do I have a prayer request for you?"

Betsy listened to Dillon's explanation of her laundry lollapalooza. Thankfully, she left out where the crime happened and what the person wore. Instead, she ended with, "I'd appreciate your prayers. I survived but didn't expect to speak to a detective on my first RV adventure."

Dillon clicked off her phone, and lines of weariness settled around her eyes. And the smile she'd worn during her vlog vanished. "I've heard of crazed fans doing bizarre things, but if I wrote the script on this one, I'd say it's the weirdest story I'd ever written."

"Might be someone seeking fifteen minutes of fame." Rose doodled on a sticky note left on the table. "Dillon, you've read about them. They do their stunt, and if no one gets hurt, the police will reprimand them, and your mystery is solved. And then we'll be able to head to Asheville."

"I hope it's as quick as you say. I heard Detective Wilds tell you he'd keep us informed. It's all we have for the time being. For me, I'm going to put in my earbuds and work on my mystery novel."

Dillon's mention of the word "mystery" reminded Betsy of the questions she had about the writer. *We don't have a clue about her. It might be all hype on her author page to sell more books. Was it such a good idea to invite her on this journey?*

IT'S A MYSTERY...BIRDS

CHAPTER FOUR

Later that afternoon, Rose and Betsy left Dillon to her novel and scoured the campground for clues. The only items found—blades of grass. Rosie carried them inside the RV, and Bets decided to call her hubby to tell him what had happened earlier in the day.

"You saw a dead man?"

"I didn't see him, and now we aren't even sure he or she ever existed. But trust me, Ben, there's no need for you and Larry to worry. Forensic is Dillon's forte. And she and the detective will figure it out."

"Hon, you're on speaker, and Lar has started hyperventilating." Ben took a deep breath of his own, and Betsy knew what the love of her life's next words would be, "And why haven't you called us before now?"

"Too much around here kept me busy. When you see us the next time, we'll be super sleuths." Betsy rambled on as if she'd left the station and chugged up a steep mountain. *I think I can convince them. I think I can convince them. I think—*

"Bets, this is a job for the police. They frown upon people who snoop around crime scenes."

"Technically, there's not a crime scene. It's Dillon's word they're going on. And, yes, we're okeedokie, so you can quiet what's swirling around in your head. You don't have to drive four hours to save us again. As I said, we're fine."

"We can be in the dually and on the highway before you can say Tallahassee, Florida," Larry yelled into the phone. "Baby misses her Mama and wants to see her. And I'm missing my Rosebud too."

"Lar, Rosie is too busy investigating with Dillon to see you if you came – which you aren't. They're examining a blade of grass, which she pulled from the yard at the back door of the laundry room."

"Tell her to call me. Her side of the story tends to be more interesting."

"Larry, as surprising as it sounds, except for her usual dramatics, Rose's tale will match mine. It's the weirdest thing I've ever been a part of." Her last words jolted Betsy's memory again of the strange man in the hat. Ben must have forgotten it too. "Guys, I'll talk to you soon."

Betsy stowed her phone away and joined her friends in the camper. "Is the grass shedding any light on who our criminal is?"

"Not yet, but we're getting closer." Rose returned to the task in front of her. "Dillon, this blade is lighter in color. Is it anything?"

Her friend's last statement, coupled with the insanity of watching two grown women as they observed a section of the lawn through a magnifying glass, amused Bets. "You cannot be serious. What is a piece of grass going to tell us?"

"Nothing if you're not quiet."

"Oh, so a section of sod is speaking to us now, Rose?

I'm out of here. Anyone hankering for a snack from the office? I'm hungry for chocolate chip cookies and a soda."

When neither lady raised their head or answered Betsy, she slipped out the door and followed the path. "I'll bring them a package of cookies, and they'll put this investigation aside. Rosie can't refuse her favorite brand of soft, chewy cookies."

Betsy rounded a corner but stopped when a man ahead of her dropped a piece of paper and kept walking. The bright, yellow color caught her eye and caused her blood pressure to rise. Bets stooped and picked up the trash.

She stuck the paper in her pocket, and unsavory thoughts about the litterer made her want to chase the culprit. But common sense won the battle, and Betsy quit her grumbling about the man when she entered the office/store.

"If I can help you with anything, my name is Sandra."

"Thank you. I'm getting snacks for my traveling buddies." Betsy pulled three small bags of cookies and assorted chips off the end cap and wished she'd snagged a basket on the way in to hold her intended purchases.

Juggling all the goodies, plus her purse, deemed impossible when the strap fell off her shoulder and down her arm. The variety of goodies flew through the air. Somehow, the cashier caught them in midair.

"Here. These baskets are so much easier to manage your merchandise."

"I appreciate your help." Betsy took it and continued searching for all kinds of treats for her dedicated crime-solvers. On the last aisle, Bets spotted the tag for moon pies, but the shelf lay empty. "Sandra, do you have any moon—"

"I keep those savory delights behind the counter. Safe and secure." Sandra laid a half dozen out in front of her. "How many do you want?"

"Those will do." Betsy reached into her purse for her debit card.

"Put your card away. Whatever you want, it's on the house. Dillon, and the two of you, deserve an extra amount of comfort food for what has gone on today." Sandra bagged the food and handed it to Betsy.

"We can't take all of this for free. It cost you to buy the items." Betsy reached for her wallet a second time.

"Trust me. It's on the house. I still can't believe someone would pull a stunt like what happened this morning at this establishment."

The older woman's last sentence didn't match her relaxed expression. Betsy slipped on her detective hat and asked the cashier, "Have you ever had to call the police on other people who have vanished?"

~~~

Bets hurried to the RV with all the goodies she'd collected. And maybe a clue – if you called Sandra's coughing fit suspicious. But when Betsy opened the RV door, she forgot the cashier and asked, "Where does someone get a sheet of poster board? I haven't been gone that long."

"Sit. Sit. Sit." Rose patted the seat next to her. "And about the poster board. I tucked it under your bed months ago. I bought it to write you a note while going down the road, but Larry told me I couldn't."

"Lar is a smart fellow."

"So is Dillon. Brilliance is her new name. Come over here and behold all the clues we've written down. We are on the trail of finding out who's responsible for this.

Betsy, I've missed my calling. Police work is my next profession."

To appease her friends, Bets surveyed the humungous piece of cardboard leaning against the couch. Dillon even had it color-coded. Red for most important, down to yellow for least likely to be anything.

The patch of grass fell in the last category, which didn't surprise Betsy. She remained quiet and took another glance at the whole board and the details the two women had written on it.

"Per her usual MO, Dillon, we've lost her." Rose gestured in Betsy's direction. "And now, if she'll move to the couch, we can dig into the spoils of her trip to the office. The snacks are speaking to me."

"I'm ignoring you, Rosie, but if you're not aware, Dillon, you have the outline of a novel here. What an ideal premise for the book you can write after you finish the one you're working on."

The mystery author stared at the board and a slight frown formed on her lips. "Ladies, I've been lying to you. I'm not working on my next book. Writer's block has me stressed out, and it's so bad, dead people are showing up on laundry room floors." Dillon laid her head on the table.

Rose dropped the food bag and hurried to the author's side, getting as close to her as possible. Betsy realized she had to intervene. "If you scoot one more inch, you'll be on Dillon's lap. Focus on the moon pie in your hand, so we can find a cure for what's ailing our friend."

"It's been problematic for about six months. And now this."

"For the time being, let's forget about the disappearing man or woman. We'll get back to them later." Betsy tapped the poster board. "Can you see the possibilities, Dillon? You've painted a storyline here."

Stretching the truth a tad caused Betsy to cough, which reminded her of Sandra's reaction in the office. But she'd save her news for later. Right now, the world-famous author required a jolt of inspiration to jumpstart her wavering talents onto the blank page.

~~~

The three women brainstormed Dillon's next novel until the wee hours of the morning. About her writer's block – they'd slayed the beast. And they polished off the goodies Betsy brought from the office.

At 7:45 the next morning, Betsy woke with a cramp in her leg. "Anyone up yet? 'Cause I'm coming down off my perch. ASAP."

"Get the coffee brewing," came from the couch.

"Will do." Betsy's leg pain persisted as she attempted to locate the ladder with her toes. When she found it, she climbed down and asked, "I'm going to the bathhouse. Anyone want to join me?"

A resounding "no" came from the couch and the back bedroom, giving her the answer she expected. And on Betsy's way out the door, she flipped on the coffee maker and headed to the showers.

As she neared the bathhouse/laundry room, her steps became a bit more tentative. Dillon's predicament sat fresh in her mind as she entered. Tape still prohibited residents from using the washers and dryers. *But I'm happy no dead bodies lay on the floor this morning.*

Betsy entered the extra-large tiled shower, and her tiredness evaporated as the streams of hot water washed over her. Later, as she dried off, she glanced at the mirror. "Yep, fruits and veggies are on the menu? Ah huh! Sweets – especially the amount I consumed last nig—"

"Girl, you choose the strangest places to talk to yourself." Rose's voice echoed through the bathroom door. "Dillon and I figured it was safe for us to take our showers. We didn't see you running back to the RV screaming. Are you getting done in there?"

She opened the door a sliver. "I'm in the process, but I have to ask – did you have your ear pressed on all the doors until you found mine?" Betsy zipped her capris. "And if you wait until I'm done, one of you can use this stall."

"No need. Two rooms opened up, so we have our pick."

She finished drying her hair and gathered her belongings. She made it to the RV and had one foot on the step when she heard a noise. It came from behind a grouping of trees. Betsy, go *inside. It's your imagination playing tricks on you again – it's nothing—*

A cracking sound met her ears as if someone stepped on a limb. Bets scrutinized the grove of trees. "I can tell myself, "nothing" is out there, but it's time to call the office."

"Restorative Campground and Cabins. Florence speak—"

"This is Site 222. Something strange is going on here." Betsy filled the receptionist in on the rest. As she recounted it, a chill ran down her back. "Can you send someone to check out the area?"

"I'll do one better. Detective Wilds drove in right when you called. I'll send him over."

"Thank you." Bets texted Rose and Dillon to cut their showers short.

The detective arrived and approached the grove of trees. Even though daylight streamed through the branches, the man aimed his flashlight into the area. She watched him lean down and pick something off the ground and look at it.

Bets wanted to ask why the piece of paper held his attention for so long, but her friends arrived in their robes and towel-donned head. Finally, Rose spoke up. "Sir, whatever it is you're reading, better be important. Soap is dribbling into my eyes."

"Sorry, Rosie, in my estimation – yours is a minor inconvenience. Whoever was in the trees just scared the cock-a-doodle doo out of me. Ben says I have an overactive imagination, but this was real."

"I hate that the creep frightened you, but a person being in there may prove I'm not crazy. Last night, I started to doubt what I'd seen."

"Ladies, I can tell you someone was in the trees, but I don't know why or who." He held up a slip of paper. "I'll have the note analyzed to see if it's evidence, but it may be a bunch of words and I'll end up tossing it in the trash."

When the word "trash" left the detective's lips, Betsy recalled the item she'd plucked off the ground on her way to the office. "Will you excuse me? I have something inside I want to share."

Betsy rummaged through the drawer where she kept her capris. She'd worn them the day before, so they'd be on top of all the others. But she stopped hunting for the supposed clue and searched Ben's side of the closet for gloves to dig the paper out of her pocket.

"What are you looking for?"

Rosie's question screamed for a curt response, which

she obliged. "Oh, I'm searching for my Uncle Jake. And why have you followed me in here? Now I'll have to snuff you out."

"Betsy, be serious."

"What I'm searching for is a pair of gloves. You have any?"

"Gloves? Larry uses latex ones when he's dumping tanks. What do you need them for?"

"You'll see."

Rose left to retrieve a pair in the underneath compartment and gave them to Betsy when she came out – capris in hand. She put on the gloves, took the note out of the pocket, unfolded it, and read it to her audience. "Words written on a page aren't always the truth."

"What does yours say, Detective?" Rose inquired.

Wilds assessed the paper in his hand again, turning it over two or three times. Even from a distance, Betsy guessed the yellow color matched. And they both had a logo on the top of the page.

The man remained silent, so Rosie inched closer to him. "Sir, you can withhold your answer from us, but I've watched plenty of crime shows, and your answer to my question will be, 'it's evidence, and I'm keeping the information under wraps.' Am I correct?"

"No, it is two pieces of paper, which are most likely an item someone discarded. I appreciate the care your friend took in wearing gloves. I will take them with me to check for fingerprints. But unless the person acts out again, we have to find more leads to move forward."

"But..."

"Ms. McCloud, you're aware of protocol from your knowledge of criminals. I'd suggest you go enjoy St. Augustine for the next couple of days and leave the crime-fighting to me."

The detective held out his hand, and Betsy gave him the paper she'd found, but she'd taken a photo of it while inside the RV. She'd heard investigators on occasion lost evidence, and she wanted to safeguard the words she'd read on the slip of paper.

~~~

They took the detective's advice and rode the trolley to visit the numerous sites of St. Augustine. The day pass gave them access to their on-and-off service. At one stop, the driver suggested, "Eat at Jo Jo's Shrimp and Cheese Grits. Bon Appetit!"

"Thanks for the recommendation. Girls, come on. I'm yearning for a stick-to-your-ribs Southern dish like my mama used to make." Betsy exited the mode of transportation and waited at the curb.

"You can't be serious. The third moon pie I consumed at midnight is still keeping me company. And, it's not inviting any more food in." Rose hopped off the trolley and headed past Bets and straight to the restaurant's front door and opened it.

"Thought you weren't hungry?" Betsy questioned her friend.

"I'll find a little something to nibble on." She took Dillon's arm and entered the establishment. "And don't you be down in the dumps. Detective Wilds instructed us to lay our troubles down and have a fun day. And it begins right now."

The waiter placed menus in front of them, and within a minute or two, Rosie called him back to their table. All three ordered an entrée and dessert. While they waited, discussion of the notes ensued, and Betsy asked, "Dillon, do the words on the paper I read sound familiar?"

"I can't say I've ever seen or heard them before, but it's like the person is giving us a coded message." Dillon stirred sugar into her sweet tea.

"I planned to Google it, but the driver stopped too soon." Betsy unfolded her napkin. "Words fascinate me – are these part of a poem? A play? Maybe a movie?"

"Or they are their own words." Rosie drummed her fingers on the table. "I so much wish Mr. Wilds would have spilled what was on his paper. Bets, you should have told him, 'I'm not telling you what's on mine until you tell me what yours says.'"

"This is why you're not an investigator, Rosie." Betsy stole a drink from her friend's soda and regretted it. Oh, how she longed to spit it out. When she finally swallowed, she sputtered out, "I forgot you ordered regular tea. Blah!"

"Serves you right for slobbering on my glass."

"Rose, you crack me up. And I'm so glad the Lord put you two ladies in my life. At such a time as this."

"It's funny how our heavenly Father works, and He's handling this too – whatever the outcome. But there's a possibility…" Betsy halted because her next words, if air hit them, implied Dillon might have brought the shenanigans on herself.

"Go ahead and say whatever it is. I can take it."

"Dillon, I don't know why, but I get the feeling the person knows you. Even if we know what my note says, the other one – and I'm assuming here - has to have wording on it too. And they were both on yellow paper and the same size sheet. What is your favorite color?"

She sipped her tea and appeared to reflect on Betsy's question. When she set the glass on the table, she said, "It is yellow, which may be a coincidence. But what gives you the impression this person knows me? I'm not tracking with you."

"My note has a feminine flair to the words." Betsy brought out her phone. "See. The letters are closer to calligraphy than normal text. A serial killer isn't going to take the time to write, 'Words written on a page aren't always the truth.'"

"Let me try to make sense of what you said." Rose cupped her chin in her hand. "So, Bets, you're leaning towards this being someone from Dillon's past, and they have followed her to a campground in upstate Florida? How would they know which campground we'd choose?"

"As illogical as it sounds, my gut tells me it's a crazed admirer. They don't have to be from her past. Look at you – you commandeered your RV, signed up for a writer's conference, and talked Dillon into this trip. Hey, maybe it's you parading as a fanatic fa—" Laughter stole Betsy's last word.

"Mrs. Stevenson, you can laugh all you want. The Lord has this handled. And He's going to give us and the detective clues to figure out who it is. And, for the record, it is not me. I don't wear frilly underwear on my bottom. And I wouldn't be caught dead with them on my head."

"Ladies, I can't wait for my vlog later this afternoon."

~~~

The three somehow got through their meal without one of them choking, and after one too many rounds of merriment, the women pushed their plates away. Betsy caught their waiter, "Can you bring us to-go containers and a bag?"

The waiter picked up their plates. "Do you want me

to box up the dessert, as well?"

"Does a chicken crow at sunrise? Oh, I mean rooster. I had my sexes mixed up."

"Rosie, all of us know what you meant, but it'd be interesting to see if a chicken's cackling could wake a person. Next time I'm on a farm, I'll take a nap and find out."

"Ladies, it's time to go. We've entertained the staff and patrons long enough." Dillon stood and pushed in her chair.

Rose carried the bag out of the restaurant. "I wonder if the waiter put forks in for our desserts? I plan to eat them somewhere in our travels. Oh, here's our ride. We're on our way to Ponce De Leon's Fountain of Youth.

They boarded the trolley, and Betsy welcomed the light breeze blowing through the opened windows, making the humid day in Florida bearable, "I will say, this is the life. No agendas, except solving a pesky mystery."

"And, I, Rose Wilford, hope to crack the case, but right now – I'm eager for a drink from the Fountain of Youth. The potion promises a more youthful appearance. It may help my sagging jowls too."

Betsy regarded her friend's attempt at holding her jaw taut. "I do see, Rosebud. And, the only solution to our multiple chins and droopy jaws is Jesus' triumphant return. Or a complete nip and tuck. No water will lift these cheeks of ours."

"We're here, and you're a party pooper."

The speaker above their heads crackled. "The trolley stops here every half hour, so please enjoy your stay at the Ponce de Leon's Fountain of Youth Archaeological

Park. If you haven't bought your tickets, they're available under the arch."

Rose, Betsy, and Dillon exited the trolley, along with most of the other occupants, and purchased tickets. Then they meandered along the path under a canopy of trees covered with moss. Peacocks, with their iridescent plumage, offered a show to those who stopped to watch.

"The brochure says they do live history re-enactments. It's not too far from here." Betsy turned the map over to locate the words, "You are he—"

"Boom!"

Dillon pointed at the map Betsy held. "That'd be the cannon going off at the re-enactment."

"Thank you for letting me know. And if I didn't have a heart problem, I do now." Rose placed her hand on her chest.

"No time to dawdle, Mrs. Wilford." Betsy handed the folded map to Dillon and hugged Rosie.

Her friend backed away. "Why are you hugging me?"

"No reason, but it should hold you for the rest of the day." Betsy loved Rosie's facial expressions after receiving unexpected hugs. As far as her friend was concerned – they solved whatever troubled you in life. "And I agree with her."

Dillon appeared perplexed and said, "Agree with what?"

"Dear, you haven't been around us very long, but Betsy likes to talk to herself. Today, she had a conversation in her head, and part of it fell out of her mouth. Those listening don't have any idea what she said. Betsy, you can explain it better than I can."

She opened her mouth to share her inner discussion, but a younger man interrupted her, "You two remind me of my grandmothers."

"Boom! Boom! Boom!"

When the noise quieted, Rose said, "Betsy, don't you find it apropos a cannon exploded at the exact moment we are referred to as old women?" A loud snort came out of her for everyone within earshot to hear, and apparently, the ruckus caused a peacock to squawk too.

Betsy couldn't resist a jab. "Rose, you either scared the bird with the noise you made, or it agrees with the young man's assessment of us."

He blushed, and it carried clear down to the neck of his polo shirt—the very same shirt that announced he guided tours at the park where they visited. "Can we please start this conversation over?"

"Sure, but first I have to tell you, if you have grandmothers like them – you have a blessed life." Dillon giggled. "These two women invited me to tag along on an RV adventure, and I'm having a blast. However, it's been a little bit more interesting than planned."

"Boy howdy, has it ever come with more action than two old broa—"

"He gets we're slapping ancient. And, he's not interested in our monkey business. The guests came to hear his spiel, which would be me. Come on." Betsy examined his name tag. "Danny, take us on the tour and tell us everything you know."

For the next half hour, their tour guide shared stories of the explorer and filled their heads with more history than the ticket price promised. And the occasional BOOM kept the crowd alert.

But when Rosie plopped down at a picnic table, Betsy guesstimated her friend had succumbed to the heat.

Danny rushed to her side with water, and she said, "You go on ahead with the tour. This bag is whispering sweet nothings to me. I must answer it."

The tour continued without them, and Rose tore into the tied bag, which exposed a Styrofoam container with writing on the lid. "Look. The waiter wrote the name of the delights in script lettering. Such pretty handwriting from a man."

Betsy contemplated the lettering for less than a second. "Ladies, we may have another clue. I've waffled on whether our perpetrator is a male or female, and this package proves it could be either."

"Good point. And the writing is similar to the note you took a picture of. Could our waiter be our culprit?" Rose tapped the spoon on the table. "After I finish eating this deliciousness, we're going back to Jo Jo's."

"The person is not following us around, Rose. There's no way he or she is lurking at every stop we make. Furthermore, as you said earlier, the Lord is taking care of us."

"She's right. We're getting paranoid. Let's settle down and enjoy our desserts." Dillon grabbed a spoon and plunged into her chocolate cake.

"I'm with her." Betsy devoured half of the best key lime pie she'd ever tasted. "You two have to try a bite of this."

They tasted the others' desserts and complimented their choices. When they finished, Dillon gathered the containers and deposited them in a trash container nearby. "Since our tour is over, how about we move on, and one of you tell me the funniest adventure you've had so far in your travels?"

While they strolled around the fifteen-acre park,

Betsy shared their humorous stories from Biloxi, Mississippi. "Winnie B came out of that stop, and Rosie's lessons on how to drive it too, which I'm sure you've noticed – is still a work in progress."

"I'm an expert driver. And, the reminder of our stop there brings me back to the subject of gorgeous penmanship. Our perp may have excellent handwriting, but our friend, Linda Richeson, makes signs that shout "Hallelujah" when you read them. We also found the idea for Sassy Seconds *Two* in Biloxi."

Betsy added to Rosie's story, "All of us loved our pit stop in the Magnolia State."

"Back up. What is a Sassy Seconds *Two*?" Dillon squinted her eyes shut as if the inquiry hurt.

"When we finally made it to Florida, Larry and I bought a place and named it after Linda's shop, Sassy Seconds. We added a *Two* at the end. Right now, the roof is in the process of getting repaired."

"Which reminds me, when we finish our tour of St. Augustine, we have to check in with our hubbies. They probably think the thug has kidnapped us and tied us to chairs in a basement. And, the ransom note is pending delivery to our families."

"Betsy, two problems arise from what you just said. First, the criminal, or criminals, don't know where we live. Or I hope they don't. The other issue with delivering the note – they don't have our email address."

"Dillon, listening to you two makes it such a joy to hang around with published authors." Rose linked arms with Betsy. "And for your information, not every incident—minuscule to major—has to turn our thoughts back to the person who might be stalking Dillon."

"Rosebud, it keeps our minds fine-tuned on details we

may have missed. But I do have to comment on the poster board you and Dillon put together. It's definitely a foundation to build on for her next novel, but you have to admit a blade of grass is a tad farfetched."

"And saying the perpetrator has a way of finding our husbands' contact information isn't?"

Betsy yawned. "Isn't it time to catch the trolley and head back to the campground? I want to give Ben a call, then relax in the hot tub."

"Not so fast." Dillon held up the brochure. "We have one more attraction, which is on Rosie's bucket list from the beginning of our travels. It's time we dip our cups in the 'special' water and see if it renews us."

"The thought of tasting H_2O from a spring discovered six hundred plus years ago doesn't sound as appealing as it once did." Rose scrunched up her nose. "I'm going to trust the Lord will make all things new when He calls me home."

CHAPTER FIVE

The campground came into view, and Dillon announced, "When we get to the RV, I'm going to do my vlog. Then I'll tackle a scene in my book that's been giving me fits. Afterward, I am going to take a nap."

She hadn't kicked them out, but Bets suggested she and Rose take a hike around the grounds. "We can call Ben and Larry while we're walking. They may give us insight into where to start our search."

But the call never materialized because, in less than three minutes, Rosie directed Betsy's eyes to a patch of dirt near the laundry room's rear door and said, "I'm going back to the RV and get a tape measure. While I'm gone, take some pictures. They might be a clue."

"Or, it's the spot the two of you pulled up the grass yesterday."

"Oh, Ha! Ha! I'll be right back. Take shots of different angles while I'm gone." Rose strode in the direction of her RV.

While Betsy waited, the late afternoon sun caused rays of light to shine through the towering palm trees. Instead of taking pictures of the supposed evidence, Bets took a dozen of the lingering sunset. She hoped they'd turn out as stunning as they did in person.

She walked past the laundry room door and continued her photo sessions of the stunning sunset. "Photography is in my blood. One of these days, I'm—"

"I'm back."

Betsy bobbled her phone, and it sailed through the air, landing right next to the bare spot Rosie asked her to photograph.

"While you're down there, picking up your phone, can you snap a few photos?" Rosie slapped her knee. "I'm so funny sometimes."

"You are, and why not?" Betsy aimed her camera at the bare patch and took a few pictures. When she finished, she said, "Let's go find the maintenance man and ask him if he's worked back here in the last couple of days."

They took a shortcut through empty camping spots and found him in the shed. He stood with his back to them, working on something on his bench. And depending on what he held in his hand, Bets did not fancy startling him. In her quietest voice, she said, "Hello."

Rose whispered, "I was standing right next to you and didn't hear what you said. A little louder, please."

Bets yelled, and the man spun around. The hammer fell from his hand to the dirt floor. He left it lying there.

"We are so sorry we startled you." Betsy stepped into the shed. "Can you tell us if you've dug any holes behind the laundry room in the last two or three days?"

"No. The last hole I dug was next to our first cabin. We had a water leak. Why are you asking?"

"Can't divulge any information. It's official business.

Can we borrow one of your shovels?" Betsy surveyed the tools on a pegboard but no shovel hung there. "We promise to return it when we're done."

The broad-shouldered man shrugged and took the tool out of a cabinet. Fresh mud fell from the blade.

Betsy snatched the shovel and headed to the door. But on her way out, she noticed Rose as she edged closer to the man. "Sir, I don't mean no disrespect…but my daddy told me to clean my—"

"Extraordinary advice under different circumstances, Rose. Let's go." Bets drug her friend out the door and towards their intended target.

"You can let go of me at any time."

"And have him hear more nonsense? This is the time for fewer words and more action." She loosened the grip on her friend's sleeve. "Is that better?"

Rose gave no response, but her fingers 'zipped' her mouth shut. Betsy appreciated the silence. It gave her time to plot their next move, but conflicting thoughts nagged at her as they approached the spot. *Lord, when did we start working in the Twilight Zone?*

"Girl, whatever is the holdup? Hand me the filthy shovel. It's time to solve me a mystery."

"I've decided to return it. The detective advised us to call him if we found anything of interest. As attention-getting as this is, tampering with evidence is not important enough for us to get arrested. Who would come and visit us in jail?"

"Ben and Larry. And I won't be in the slammer, but as of right now – you are a spoilsport. Yes, it's a teensy tiny illegal. And a smidge into the gray area. And, now I've lost you. What are you staring at down there? Is there one of those flying cockroaches on the ground?"

"No, we're safe from airborne bugs," Bets assured her, but while Rosie jabbered about creepy crawly things, she eyeballed the grassless spot and concluded the shovel had dug the hole they stood over.

Betsy also realized the handle she held might possess fingerprints. She dropped the shovel and started to call the detective but stopped when she saw Dillon strolling across an occupied campsite. "Rosie, it's time—"

"For a meeting with Dillon. Our first lesson is to teach her camper etiquette. Apparently, she's not aware it's impolite to trudge through another person's spot."

"And it better be SOON." Betsy pointed. "That gentleman in 277 shot out of his chair when she trespassed. And I'm to assume it was to give Dillon a piece of his mind. However, he left his walker behind."

"I'm on it and will help him back to his seat."

While Rose assisted the older man and reseated him without incident, Betsy spied the detective's unmarked vehicle in front of the office. He marched to the spot next to the laundry room with Dillon at his heels.

"Glad you saved me a phone call. I—"

"I don't know where the shovel came from, but hand it to me." Detective Wilds held out his hand.

"Sir, I got it from the maintenance shed, and as far as I'm concerned – it's evidence. Before I dropped it, I checked the blade with the size of the hole, and it's a match. With my limited knowledge in forensics, you'd better bag it…so no one else's fingerprints get on it."

"Fine." The detective walked to his vehicle and obtained a shovel and a handful of plastic bags out of the trunk. He returned and took photos, then started to dig next to the laundry room.

He brought out four shovelfuls and checked through

them. Nothing. But on the fifth one, he stopped. Among the clumps of dirt, it appeared he'd dug up pieces of clothing. Betsy's mind raced. *Is it the frilly undies and shorts Dillon told us about?*

The detective put gloves on and removed the items he'd unearthed, placing them in the plastic bag he'd brought. Wilds then moved to the shovel lying on the ground and shoved it in another bag.

"Sir, we've stayed quiet through all of this, but I'm dying to know – can DNA and/or fingerprints be found on clothing after they've been buried then soaked by the sprinkler system?"

"It makes it harder, but it's possible."

"Detective, we're still missing the shirt and ukulele." Dillon knelt next to the hole. "I'm not the authority here, but have you dug down deep enough?"

"I tapped on what may be the sprinkler line. Another scoop into the hole, and I'll break it. Ms. McCloud, this solves part of the mystery. Now we have to find the person who wore the clothes and used the shovel to hide them."

"Glad we found some of the stuff. Now Dillon can quit thinking she's nuts."

The detective acknowledged Rosie with a nod and acted as if he had more to say, but his phone rang. He ventured to the other side of the building to take the call. Betsy positioned herself to listen but stayed in the shadows.

No words on Detective Wilds end of the call made sense. Maybe he spoke another language to the person to disguise his message to his informant. *But, on the other hand, perhaps I'm the one going bonkers, and I'm making something out of nothing.*

While Bets mulled over the officer's unrecognizable verbiage, he rejoined the other two ladies. She slinked away from her hiding place without calling attention to herself and stood with them.

"Ms. McCloud, I'll be in touch, but I'll be straight with you. I'm still leaning toward this being a prank. He or she hasn't made any other moves – it may be a one-time occurrence. There's still a missing piece—the body. We have to find the person responsible, but locating the clothes will help."

"What about the notes he or she left? Anything on them yet?"

"Dillon, I'm curious about those too." Rose pressed her index fingers together as if she prayed. "Sir, on CSI—"

"CSI is fiction." The detective removed his sunglasses and polished them on the handkerchief from his back pocket. "Ladies, the notes are being processed as we speak. So please don't worry. Let the professionals handle it."

From Dillon's wide-eyed expression, Betsy assessed her writer friend wished to kick the 'professional" out of the campground with the boots she had on. But, in the end, she said, "The mystery writer in me tells me - even if the body disappeared – it's still a crime."

"It is, and you three have already helped with finding a clue today. I'll talk to you in a day or two." The detective took the evidence bags, returned to his car, and drove away.

He's full of more bologna than an Oscar Mayer wiener factory. Betsy giggled at her obscure thought and had no idea where it came from. Again, her friends gave her a sideways glance. Neither asked what tickled her this time.

Dillon's phone buzzed, and Betsy heard her mention her boyfriend's name. "Rosie, she'll be awhile, explaining what's going on. Let's go fill in the hole Wilds left." *And search for other treasures—if any are out there.*

On their way to the area, Rosie mentioned offhandedly, "You do know we can't fill the hole?"

"Why?"

"He took the shovel." Rosie laughed out loud. "But let me help. I'll go get something we can use to accomplish the task."

Betsy stayed near the pile of dirt for no apparent reason but for grins – she snapped some pictures of the spot in question. Within five minutes, Rose returned carrying a medium-sized shovel.

"I've been thinking, Bets, you and the detective lean toward this being a hoax, but those notes are telling me otherwise. How about we go to the police station and nose around?"

"You know they won't let you within a mile of the place."

"Let me finish. As John Buchan said in a quote I saw on Facebook, 'Every man, at some point in their lives, wants to be a detective.'" This is me. Clear to my bones. Betsy. I've found my calling."

"Give me the shovel, and while I'm digging, I'll give you my diagnoses of what you have. It's heartburn or a flare-up of your IBS. Detective work isn't your mission in life. What is, is you helping people on the road and at Sassy Seconds *Two.* Anyway, you're too old to enter the Police Academy."

"They may have a special unit designed for women

our age."

"And it's called the Official Donut Lady." Betsy finished filling the hole and patted down the top, calling it good. "Time to tell the maintenance man about his confiscated shovel. Not sure how he'll take it."

They walked to the tool shed and the man stood in the same place they'd left him. Bets opened her mouth to explain the unreturnable tool, but her vision clouded over. Blinking a dozen times didn't change what she saw. *A UKELELE HANGING ON THE WALL. He's our guy.*

~~~

"Rosie, we have to find Dillon!" Betsy skedaddled in the direction of the RV, not waiting for her friend, and imagined the maintenance man had picked up the hammer – and chased after them. "Can you hurry?"

"As I've said before – my short legs don't run. I'm also carrying the shovel. Stop moving, or I'm going to keel over."

Betsy came to a halt and dialed the detective's number. He answered, and between her excitement and trying to catch her breath, she hollered into the phone, "Sir, get yourself back here. Another critical piece of evidence has materialized. We've found the ukulele."

She hung up and called Dillon. "There's no time to explain. Meet us at the shed behind the office."

~~~

Dillon arrived at the same time as the detective, and together they walked into the shed. Betsy and Rose followed them into the cramped space. Wilds huffed, and Bets assumed it had to do with the crowd assembled around him.

"Excuse me, but before we get this interrogation

underway, I have to ask everyone to scooch your foot a tiny bit to the left. Someone is grinding my little toe into the dirt."

Movement from everyone in the room must have provided relief since Rose sighed and then added, "Sir, you can proceed with your grilling."

"No one is grilling anyone." The detective took his hat off. "Mark, if these women haven't informed you, the ukulele you have hanging on the wall is evidence in Ms. McCloud's case. Please wait in the office until I'm done here."

"What about them?" He pointed at the ladies as he inched toward the door.

"Even if I asked them to leave, they won't. Go on ahead. I'll be there soon."

Mark lingered at the door a moment then continued through it. Betsy and her friends' attention moved from him and zeroed in on the detective. He put gloves on and lifted the ukulele off the hook, examining it for an extended length of time.

"You can take all the time you need. We're not going anywhere."

"Dillon is correct. We're stuck to you like a bee to honey. How about you quit wasting time and do what you're paid to do?"

Rosie's gumption on the speed of the man's work surprised Betsy, and it took all of her faculties not to laugh. But one glance at the detective broadcasted, "We're on our way to the slammer."

Wilds removed a pouch from his jacket and made eye contact with each of the ladies. "If you stay, which I'm not happy about, I'll say this once. DO NOT touch anything. If you do, I'll arrest all of you."

If any of them breathed after his warning, they only took short intakes to stay alive. Betsy, as well as Dillon and Rose, kept their eyes on the man. Like a master, he twirled the brush across the fine grain of the ukulele, checking for fingerprints.

The wall clock ticked away, filling the stillness. Betsy's neck began to ache, and she prayed he'd hurry. No sooner had the thought entered her mind, he laid the instrument on the workbench. "I don't find any prints. Now, if you'll excuse me, I have official police business to do. You cannot be in the room any longer."

"Rosebud, this concludes the single bit of police work you'll get to do today." Betsy joked about her friend's supposed calling, but no one seemed amused. *Guess you had to be there.* "Okay, then. Can we go to the RV? I'm hungry."

Dillon and Rose agreed with her peckiness, and they made their way to the door. But stopped when the detective spoke again. "Don't leave the campground. I will talk to you after I speak with Mark."

"Sir, if you don't find us at the RV, we'll be wandering around the park."

"But I'm hungry." Bets whispered to the ladies, but when Rosie jabbed her in the ribs, she caught her friend's exuberant hint. "Yep, that's what we'll be doing."

The three strolled toward the RV but veered off to the back row. A row of palm trees swayed in the ocean breeze. An idyllic sight until Bets spied a mound of dirt off behind the last campsite. "Someone has been poking around in here. We better call the det—"

"Not this time."

"Dillon, if you get us arrested – I'll still buy your books." Betsy put her hand over her nose. "I'm not hungry anymore. And no one with half a brain is hiding anything in there. "Pooey!"

"It may stink, but it's prime real estate for hiding evidence." Dillon grabbed a rake and bucket next to the pile and began scraping leaves and other debris away. Within a minute or two, she laid the rake down. "If a pigsty smells this bad, I don't want to work at one. However, here is my paycheck for the dirty work."

"What is it?"

The author, using the rake, pulled the missing Hawaiian shirt out of the compost pile. "Ladies, it's time to call the detective. He may haul us in, but from my vantage point – we're doing all of his work."

Bets touched base with Officer Wilds, and they met him at the maintenance shed. Rose carried the shirt on the rake out in front of her the whole way, which amused Betsy. But the stench almost overtook her. "Are everyone's eyes watering?"

"Ten-four."

"Good buddy."

Her two friends uttered CB lingo, and Betsy would wager Dillon knew far less about the radio system than Rosie. But their exchange cracked her up until she witnessed the detective's humorless expression when he relieved Rose of the evidence she carried.

"The St. Augustine Police Department prides itself in the work we do on a daily basis in our fine city. We do not appreciate when people involve themselves in active crime scenes. There's a good possibility you've damaged the case."

Under normal circumstances, if a man with a badge reprimanded you, you'd beg for mercy. But witnessing his antics as he stuffed the shirt into the gallon-size bag and the subsequent splitting of it brought laughter from the ladies.

"Whatever you're chuckling about better cease and desist. It's getting late, and I'd love to see my family sometime today."

"Yes, Sir." All three ladies chimed in.

"Good. First off, Ms. McCloud, although you located this without a warrant – it's evidence, if you identify it as the shirt in question, I can proceed."

"It's the one. I'm a hundred percent sure. Are you convinced it's a crime now, or do we have to—"

"You have to do nothing from this point forward. Have dinner. Relax. Write a book. But no digging around the campground. I'll be in touch. And speaking of which – don't touch anything else."

"What about the maintenance man—" Betsy halted her words, realizing what her statement had implied. "Oh, I don't want to touch him, but could he be a suspect?"

"He has consented to a lie detector test, which will happen at the end of this week. However, Mark has a strong alibi. He's been at Restorative Campground for ten years. He's not our man, and I'll answer the question floating around in your head. He isn't a flight risk either."

"Say what?" Dillon hit her hand on the tool bench. "We found him with a crucial piece of evidence, and he's allowed to roam free. To be able to terrorize another woman when all she wants to do is take a shower and do laundry."

"Ms. McCloud, I understand. Everything about him and his surroundings does make him appear guilty. But what if he's the red herring in your story? Maybe he's simply a hard-working guy, struggling to feed his family."

"Fine, but can we get this done so I can enjoy my RV journey? And write my book? The way it's looking, Jesus may have to return to help us find the creep who wears undergarments on his or her head, and scares people half to death."

"I'm hoping for the Lord's return, but Dillon, you've given me an idea. We could go to Victoria's Secret and purchase a pair of lacy underwear and hang it in the laundry room. If he or she is prowling around, they won't be able to resist another tryst with the new pretties."

Betsy had never heard a funnier quip from her friend, and the others must have agreed. None of them spoke for a length of time, but when the detective regained his composure, he said, "It's okay to have a little levity, but this is serious. So please stay out of it and let me do my job."

"No more digging in stinky piles for me. It's all yours." Rosie wiped her hands on her pants.

"Correct. And you won't be here to hamper my investigation. I am releasing you to continue your travels. As long as we're in communication with each other, you're free to go." Wilds rubbed the side of his head. "Are you gone yet?"

"You don't have to tell us twice, but we'll be sure to stay in touch."

The officer exited the maintenance shed, and the ladies followed suit. However, on their way to the RV, Betsy's mind ran amok. Something about Dillon's last few words to the detective felt a little out of whack. *I don't think she's going to wait to hear from him because she's—*

Dillon's phone rang, and she put it on speaker. "Ms. McCloud, I cannot restate this enough—we must stay in touch. Please text me where you are staying each night on your way to Asheville. I feel it's a safety precaution. Goodbye."

Betsy didn't write mysteries, but his needing to know their whereabouts sounded fishy. And she asked Dillon the million-dollar question, "Since you're the expert, is it normal procedure to allow a person to leave the area when a crime has been committed against them?"

"Or ask them to divulge information on their locations at all times?" Rosie shuddered. "It's a little unnerving."

"That it is. And to answer Betsy, in all the classes I've taken, it's not okay to leave. Ladies, it's time for you to show me what RVing is all about. I'm not going to let Wilds or the person doing whatever they're doing change our plans."

~~~

"Ben, you heard me right. The detective cleared our travels, and Dillon is ready. It's late in the day, but we're hitting the highway as soon as Rose unhooks everything." Betsy toyed with the straw in her coffee mug. "Are you okay with us venturing so far?"

"You two have been trained by the best RV drivers around."

"Larry runs into poles. Somehow, this does not reassure me."

"Betsy, I meant more me than our best friend. You'll do fine. And I'm confident, in a day or two, the detective will figure out it's a hoax – as you and he thought. Go, have fun wherever you land. We'll be praying for all of you."

"We appreciate as many as you send our way. And

please tell Larry that Winnie B will return unharmed, along with his wife. Trust me on this. I haven't asked, but how are you doing? Is Matilda making sure you're eating right? Not too much Taco Bell?"

"Too much Taco Bell? How is that possible? And, yes, our pooch and I are doing fine. But, she's missing her mom."

"Give her a hug for me."

"Hon, hold on. Larry's calling me."

While Betsy waited, she caught movement outside the RV. A second glance caught the top of a person's head as they darted between the campers. She left it alone but then heard the familiar sound of one of the compartments closing. *Strange.*

"I'm back. The wedding prep for Everly and Douglas is in full swing. We hope you're planning on getting back here in a couple of weeks. If not, Everly and her aunt will hunt you down."

Ben's bantering about the future nuptials sidestepped Betsy's thoughts of someone messing with Winnie B. *I'm being unreasonable. It's a tree branch scraping the side—not anyone moving around outside Rosie's camper?*

"Did I lose you?"

"No, I'm here. Our conversation will be interrupted in 1…2…3—"

"We've dumped tanks and stowed the cord. And all outside compartments are locked. Take it from here, Dillon," Rose announced on her way in the door.

"It's official - we're on the road again. Rose, put Winnie B in gear and get these tires rolling north to Asheville."

Betsy's doubts about the noise evaporated after their

cheery announcement. They'd been the ones messing in the compartment. "Ben, I better go. And, yes, we'll be back to help with the wedding arrangements. Talk to you soon."

She stowed her phone in the cup holder at the banquette and buckled her seat belt. "Dillon, you can sit in the front seat to enjoy our travels. You can work on your novel when we arrive at our next stop. Where are we landing, Rosie?"

"P.I.T.S. is set. Our final destination tonight is Savannah. We're bypassing Atlanta. If it's okay with everyone?" Rosie tooted the horn and pulled out of the RV spot. "Oh, we can't forget to call the detective when we land."

"We'll see."

"Say what? We have to call him." Rosie's reaction to Dillon's statement matched Betsy's.

"Yes, he told us to call him, but this whole business of the man keeping track of every single step we take has me questioning his motives."

"Go on."

"Rose, your eyes do a much better job surveying the road ahead than on Dillon."

"As I was saying, what if he is the one who scared me? He answers his phone on the first ring. We can't blink twice after we call him, and he's at the campground. And he cleared the maintenance man without the promised lie-detector test."

~~~

The courtesy patrol led Winnie B through the cutest-of-cute campgrounds in Savannah. Dillon had found it on the internet, and it sat across the street from the park Detective Wilds had suggested in a text he'd sent Betsy an hour into their trip.

The towering Southern Oaks created a canopy, shading the RV, making it the perfect spot to sip their sweet tea. And, per the norm, Betsy's imagination ran wild as she opened the side compartment. She waited for someone to jump out and scare the bejeebers out of her.

Praise be to God, nothing or no one sprang forth at her. But as she shoved the umbrella out of the way, a lawn chair fell out of the compartment and hit the top of her foot. Hard! "Red alert, if anyone is interested. I've hurt myself."

Dillon had a chair open, and Betsy settled in it while Rose searched for the ice machine. Soon, her friend struggled with the twenty-pound bag of ice she'd purchased, which left Bets mystified as to why she'd purchased such a large quantity.

She left the abundance of ice to the other ladies to figure out where to store it. Her foot throbbed and had turned every color of the rainbow. *Lord, I'm not supposed to ask why, but this doesn't make a bit of sense.*

Rose took a peek. "Bets, it's time to visit an Urgent Care facility."

She shook her head, "I'm fine right here," but an attempt to wiggle her foot made her rethink her resolve. "You two will have to help me."

They did, and even though Betsy's foot screamed and she longed to cry, her friends' made her chuckle when they replicated Aaron and the other Israelite holding Moses' arms up. Her glee lasted until they'd gone the short distance to the RV door.

Three grown women found it impossible to squeeze through the small opening together, but Betsy figured it out in all their maneuvering around, "I'll sit on the step and scooch up to the floor and pull myself up onto the couch to the end that has the seatbelt."

Dillon and Rose watched her, and in no time, she'd buckled herself in. The other two occupied their seats in the front. Rosie put the RV in gear then asked, "Anything else we can do for our injured passenger?"

"Stop at the office and tell them we're still here."

Rosie drove the short distance, and Dillon ran in. A minute later, she returned. "They asked if there was anything they could do. I told them we had it handled. The woman assured me they'd hold our spot."

"Good to know." Even as frustrated as she'd ever been, Betsy knew she'd laugh about this sometime soon. But, right now, her foot h.u.r.t. *Maybe if I call Ben, he will keep my mind off the pain. And he'll pray for me.*

Or not. While Rose drove to the urgent care, Betsy's phone rang a dozen times then landed on voicemail. Her reply to her husband's witty message said, "Call me. Have more news, but it has nothing to do with Dillon McCloud's mystery."

"Bets, if what you said doesn't put a fire under his behind, nothing will. Ben is quite forgetful when it comes to his phone." Rose tapped hers clipped to the dash. "I can call Larry if you want me to?"

"No, keep driving and get me where we're going."

"Dillon, if you haven't noticed, Betsy's optimistic attitude flew out the window, and now Mrs. Grump is camped in her place. Not pretty on a good day." Rose made a left into an empty parking lot. "We've arrived."

"It's about time." Betsy smiled as her friend parked. It had taken less than ten minutes to reach their destination, and the hard part of getting her out the door began. But she had this one handled too. She slid off the couch to the floor. Thud. *Ouch! Not what I planned.*

"Are you okay?"

"Never been better, but Rosie, I need you to go to the side door and open it. Then, I'll make my way down the stairs while you get me a wheelchair. I'll be waiting for you on the bottom step. Position the chair so when I stand, I can fall into it. Copy?"

Bets heard both front doors slam shut and the side door open. Rosie shouted, "Dillon is handling the delivery of the wheelchair, so I'm ready to catch you. Come on! Heave ho. Or better yet, do as the Bible tells us in Isaiah, 'Soar on wings like eagles.'"

"Always ready with a verse. I like it. And, Rosie, I changed my mind. When the wheelchair gets here, put it next to the door and hold it still."

"I'm back, and the chair is where you want it." Dillon smiled.

Betsy's choreography, or "soaring," as her friend suggested, resembled a wounded buffalo on the plains after they landed a hoof in a gopher hole. "Yes, I do paint a picture." A giggle escaped.

"Either you tell us what's dancing in your head, or we're staying here."

"A bison fell into a hole."

"And my question is why are bison rattling around in your head at a time like this." Rose wheeled the chair toward the urgent care's door, and it automatically opened.

A young woman behind the counter asked, "May I help you?"

The second she inquired, Betsy's phone rang. "Rosie, here's my wallet with my medical card. You can answer anything they ask. Hello." Betsy listened to her hubby and grasped the fact he'd not listened to her message.

"And Larry—"

"Benjamin, my foot or buffalos in North America are not interested in what you bought at Home Depot."

"Okay, I'm lost. Guess I better listen to my messages before I call next time. Fill me in."

Bets gave him every detail, but near the end of her story, she heard a familiar sound. "Are you jingling your keys? You do not have to drive here to get me. I'll be fine after they check me out. They'll wrap it, and we'll be on our way to tour Savannah."

"I ask again – are you sure?"

"Positive." Betsy rated her confidence level at ninety-five percent, leaving the other five hidden in the chasm of her mind.

"Call me when you know more."

"I will. Love you! Don't tell my mom. Better to leave her in the dark."

"She's not home from her trip yet."

"Our worldly traveler. Bye. Talk to you soon." Betsy hung up and reclaimed her wallet from Rose. "I'll take it from here. And I'm able to wheel myself to the seating area." Sadly, she progressed less than three feet and ran into the wall with her left foot—not the one bruised already.

"I see you're an expert. I'm your driver for today."

"Maybe after Mrs. Stevenson's appointment." A nurse snuck in between Rosie and the wheelchair, and she rolled her down a long hallway. "We're going in here."

The woman wheeled her into the room and stopped next to the bed. The transition from the chair to the table resulted in Betsy muttering "ouch" more than once. But when the nurse adjusted her foot to get the right angle for X-rays, her pain level escalated to a thousand twenty-five.

"Take deep breaths. It helps. And so does talking. The paper says you're from Fort Myers. What brings you to this part of Georgia?" The woman moved her foot a little bit while she asked questions.

"Long story, but my friends and I are traveling in an RV. We're on our way to North Carolina." On purpose, Betsy left out the part about a famous author tagging along. And she had to admit the chitter-chatter helped to ease her foot pain.

"Mrs. Stevenson, we're finished here, but I have to tell you. My boyfriend and my dream are to travel in an RV. But, it'll still be a few…ah…years."

The nurse brought the wheelchair closer to the table, and Betsy spotted a hint of pink on the young lady's cheeks. She let it slide and noted the name on her tag. "Emily, don't wait too long to begin your adventure. God's creation is magnificent."

"From what I've seen, yes, it is." She helped Bets to the wheelchair then pushed her to the open door and down another hall. She inched along, then stopped and whispered in Betsy's ear. "Don't tell anyone, but we're eloping this weekend and hope to become traveling nurses by the end of the year."

"Good for you. And my lips are sealed." Betsy dug in her purse and brought out a business card, and in a hushed tone, she said, "Email or call to tell me how the newlyweds are doing. The Early Birds delight in adding another to their flock."

"Early Birds?"

"We don't have enough time for me to explain. Go to

my website. It'll tell you more than you ever wanted to know."

"On my break, I'll check it out." The nurse turned into a new room. "The doctor will be in shortly."

While Betsy waited, she scanned the room. A typical doctor's office. She glanced at the examining table in the middle of the floor—the one she'd have to figure out how to get on. *Please, Lord, let them diagnose me from where I'm sitting.*

After an extended stay in the room, Betsy determined everyone must have hurt themselves and sought care. To make the time go faster, she prayed for her new friend, Emily. At the end of her prayer, Bets thought her resounding "amen" might bring in the troops. It didn't.

She wheeled over to the magazine rack and took out a People Magazine. Upon leafing through it, she announced, "I don't know any of these peo—" A knock stopped her mid-sentence. "Come in."

Two women in white coats entered her room. One of them showed her the X-ray of her lower extremity. The doctor pointed, "You've broken the bone attached to your little toe, so surgery is not required since you aren't a runner."

How does she know what I do in my spare time?

"I'll fit you with a boot, but you must wear it for eight weeks. Ten, if it's still bothering you. Walk on your heel at all times. And keep it elevated and iced as much as possible for the next week. Any questions?"

Betsy still wanted to inquire how the doc concluded she refrained from exercising, but Rosie barged in. "We've been out there so long. Are you taking my friend to the hospital? Is there something more wrong with her than her pinky toe?"

"Rosebud, go back to the waiting room. I'm not going anywhere but back to the RV."

The doctor fitted Betsy with a boot, and she managed to make it out of the office and into the camper without needing her friends' help. *This boot is going to work.*

Rosie headed to the campground, but Betsy spotted a Taco Bell about a block from their final destination. "My spill may have altered our plans today, but I'm going to make it up to you and buy you a late dinner."

CHAPTER SIX

After their fill of tacos and burritos, Betsy settled at the banquette to play a word game on her phone. But when it buzzed, it popped out of her grasp and landed on the table, showing Ben's name. She answered, "I have my foot propped up, and I'm doing fine and dandy."

"Hope you aren't going to climb up and sleep over the cab tonight. And you are staying off of it as much as possible, right?"

"I am. Rosie is switching beds with me. I'm sure the couch is comfortable, but don't worry about me and get the roof fixed down there."

"We're on the last part, but we also have some not-so-good news to share from this end concerning Douglas. He fell off the ladder late this afternoon and bummed up his knee."

"Rose, get over here. I'm putting you on speaker. Repeat yourself."

Ben gave them the whole story, and when he finished, Rose sprang from the banquette. "What about the wedding? Douglas can't walk his bride up the aisle after the ceremony on crutches. Our group is not doing well."

"Breathe. You know what to do, and it starts with a 'P'—"

"Betsy's a hundred percent correct. Prayer is our defense. Larry, get on the phone."

"I'm here, Rosie. Pray on."

"Lord, this may be one of the longest prayers I've ever prayed, but—"

"But we'll keep her on track." Betsy heard Larry's uproarious laughter at her comment and added, "Yes, Father, You know our Rose rambles on and on and on—"

"Onward, Lord. Please send your angels down to protect the Early Birds and the people You've put in our life. As You can see, we have a huge predicament with Douglas hurting himself – and we can't forget Betsy. We need all of our appendages to accomplish what You've set in front of us to do. Clothe all of us with Your protective armor."

"And Rosie said, 'Amen.'"

"Lord, excuse Larry. I'll continue now. We know Your armor helps us stand against the enemy's schemes, but it looks like we need it to protect us when we stand, sit, walk and drive. Wherever You lead…ah…I guess I'm done. In Jesus Name. AMEN!!!"

"Goodbye, Rosie. Call me later so you can talk to Baby. She misses you."

Betsy chuckled at their friends' interchange and had her finger poised to hang up when she heard her hubby say, "You forgetting me is getting to be a habit. I'm starting to get a complex." Ben laughed.

"I did forget you. Sorry. But back to your question. I'm okay and will stay off of my foot as much as I can. Tell Douglas to do the same. I'll talk to you later."

"Be good."

"I promise." Bets clicked off her phone and heard Rose proclaim, "I've been considering some..." then silence. A sentence like this from her friend came with consequences. Now with a bum foot – she'd rather not have any more action for one day.

While Dillon pecked away on her computer, Rose cozied in next to Betsy. "Since we're here, we ought to investigate Savannah. They have the same kind of trolley as St. Augustine. Bets, we can help you get off and on. Or we can ride around the city tomorrow. You decide."

"Rose, you and Dillon, go ahead. I'm not going to be doing much hopping on and off of anything right now."

"Nooooooooooooo...nooooooooooooo...and...noooo ooooooooooo. We're not leaving you alone to mope."

"I have a better idea." Dillon closed her computer and put it on her bed. "I can see Savannah another time. I said I wasn't going, but I've never been to Fort Myers. And it sounds like you have lots going on down there. I'm dying to see your store."

"Are you sure?" Rose looked at the author over her readers. "Fort Myers can wait. You had your heart set on seeing Asheville. Heading north is sure to clear your head and end any hint of lingering writer's block."

Their conversation reminded Betsy of the hurricane discussion the year before. They had struggled with the decision of all of them going back to the Sunshine State, or Ben and Betsy traveling north for her book signings without Rose and Larry.

"I've made my decision, and I'm ready to head to Fort Myers. Betsy, you can thank me for keeping you off your foot. We'll visit Savannah next time. With Rosie's list of things to do, she'd have worn your boot out on its first outing. And…"

"And…what?"

Dillon paused and wiped her eyes. "Ashville is for another day. No point in seeing the Biltmore. I'd always dreamed of getting married in one of their gardens, but it doesn't look like it'll ever happen." She ended her announcement with a sob.

"Oh, I feel so bad. If we'd known, we'd have suggested an alternate route. Say Nashville, Tennessee. Honky-tonk, bluegrass, and authentic country-western tunes heals anything. We could see if Willie was in the hou—"

"I'll stop her gusts that threaten to blow us off course more than we already are. But. Dillon, even if Rose is babbling – we're females, and all of us envision the perfect wedding in our minds. You'll get yours. If you've prayed about this happening, the Lord will be faithful."

"The Early Birds will pray too. Our little group has a list of answered prayers from here to Bermuda and back again."

The author dried her tears on the hem of her t-shirt. "My family is scattered around the world. Normally, we're too busy to see each other. But now that I've found you two—it feels like I'm home."

"Well said, Dillon. And you haven't met the other couple who travels with us. Mary and Jeff are good people. We'll be sure to include her on our next journey. She's a lot like us, but a lot quieter."

"I'm thankful for that last piece of news, Rose."

Dillon's comment caused laughter to fill the RV. And it continued whenever one of them said anything – even if it didn't pertain to Mary. But their humor plummeted to the basement compartment when the detective's name showed on the mystery writer's silenced phone.

She answered and hit the speaker button, placing the phone in front of Rosie. "Hello, Officer. How are you? We've had a change of plans. We're heading to Fort Myers tomorrow."

"What about North Carolina?"

Betsy detected an annoyance in his tone with this new development. She also heard him take in a breath or two, which gave her the impression he had to calm down before he spoke again.

Dillon finally said, "I don't see why going south is a problem. The investigation hasn't changed locale, only the person – me – who witnessed the crime – or lack thereof. Any news on the notes we found? The shovel? Have they been analyzed for fingerprints?"

"Forensics takes time, Ms. McCloud, which you understand more than most people."

"I am fully aware of the timetable, but tomorrow we're on our way to Dayto—" Dillon shook her head and whispered, "That man infuriates me, and then I talk too much."

"Well, since you'll be going right through St. Augustine again, stop in at the resort on your way through. Another clue has shown up." He cleared his throat. "Um…the housekeeper found it yesterday."

Dillon paced back and forth from the bathroom door to the captain's chairs. "Sir, you're killing me. What are you doing? I've written mysteries for fifteen years, and I don't believe you. I smell a rotten fish in St. Augustine, Florida."

"Could it be another red herring? Or what, Ms. McCloud? You'll have to stop in and see if I'm telling the truth. Call, and I'll meet you at the campground office." The call ended.

~~~

Betsy convinced the other two the following morning they needed to go out for a late breakfast. "The drive to St. Augustine amounts to three hours and change."

Dillon gave a "yes" on her way to take her shower at the bathhouse. Then she added, "I like your way of thinking. Whatever the detective has to show us can wait." Dillon retraced her steps and stuffed a bath towel in her bag.

The second Dillon shut the door, Betsy said, "Rosie, I don't know if I'm reading something into what's going on, but if she believes he's the one who committed the crime, we don't want to spook him. Or let him know we suspect him."

"Mrs. Stevenson, you may not be a mystery writer, but you sound more like one every day."

"Thanks. My spending time with Dillon has reignited my desire to get busy with another book. Maybe I'll change genres. Do more suspense. Whodunits. James Patterson, watch out. Here I come. Oh, I better run this past Mr. Pickle. He may not appreciate the drastic change."

"If you pen murder mysteries, please do it minus the blood and guts."

"You do realize a murder often includes blood?"

"I do, but if I'm going to read your book – it has to sway towards kinder and gentler as George H. W. Bush would say. And, Betsy, you can't change what you write if you don't sit down and write."

Betsy searched for an object to inflict pain and found a hairbrush near the cupholder. She picked it up and gave Rose a gentle bop on the back of the head. Not enough force to hurt her, but plenty to get her point across. "If you haven't noticed, I'm incapacitated."

"You are, and you're going to milk it for all it's worth. Hit me again, Missy, and you'll be the next corpse on the laundry room floor with flowered undies on *your* head."

"You've heard of the show called, *Kids Say the Darndest Things*, but in your case – it's *An Old Person Says the Silliest Stuff*." Bets laughed as she laid the brush on the table.

"I'm sorry I missed whatever happened while I was gone." Dillon closed the door behind her. "Are we ready to go to breakfast, or I should say – an early lunch?"

"We are. Buckle up." Betsy adjusted her seatbelt at the banquette.

Five minutes later, Rose pulled out of the campground. GPS took them to the rental place to pick up a wheelchair then to downtown Savannah. On the third go around the block in search of a parking spot, Betsy said, "They gave me a handicap placard."

Rosie pulled Winnie B. into the ideal spot under a canopy of trees. "Hand me the placard, and I'll lay it on the dash. Bets, I hope it's okay. It's as close as I can get. Dillon, do you want the honor of pushing her, or can your bestest friend in all the world do it?"

"We have to humor her sometimes. I'm all yours, Rose. Jesus, take the wheel, or in this circumstance, the handles."

Betsy held on as Rosie weaved through Savannah's historic downtown area on their way to the restaurant. She enjoyed viewing the buildings' architecture with nothing to do but gawk, and she snapped tons of pictures.

At a stoplight, she admired the stained-glass windows, which adorned the Cathedral of St. John the Baptist.

They glistened in the mid-morning sunshine. The spires stood tall against the bright blue sky. No doubt the workers accomplished a magnificent feat of masonry in the late 1800s. *Ben would love to see this. I'll write this area on my Bucket List.*

Their travels continued, and Betsy suspected another "soar on wings like eagles" coming, but Rose cleared the curb without a mishap. They dined to their fill on home-style cooking and plenty of Southern charm to go with the delicious food at Mrs. Wilkes Dining Room.

"My dad used to sit back from the table and undo his belt when he'd eaten too much. In my case, my capris don't have anything but a zipper to let loose. I don't dare open it up. All of my wherewithals would tumble out."

Betsy's revelation made dividing the check into thirds difficult. Tears streamed down their cheeks, but they accomplished it after a dab or two at their eyes. Finally, they exited the establishment, and Dillon rolled Betsy to the RV without hitting anything or anyone.

She opened the door and helped Bets to the couch. "Ladies, this bears repeating. I love this RV lifestyle more than I ever imagined, excluding the part about Betsy's accident and not knowing who disappeared on me in St. Augustine."

"After we return the wheelchair, we'll be on our way to finding out more information on the latter." Rose dropped into the driver's seat and started the vehicle. "I don't know about you, but I'm ready to head south?"

And whatever we find out could alter or delay the rest of our trip. Betsy relaxed on the couch but kept her thoughts to herself. She'd do anything to keep Rosie from getting herself in a tither. *Safety first is the key.*

~~~

On their way to St. Augustine, Betsy had clicked on the Restorative Campground and Cabins site and checked them in. When they arrived, the courtesy patrol guided them to the same spot as their last visit.

Rose hopped out of the rig. "I'll get a chair for Betsy to sit in."

"While she's reclining in it, I'll bring her sweet tea. And, I'll text the detective and tell him we're here."

Betsy concluded, pampering agreed with her. She also enjoyed the late afternoon breeze off the Atlantic while she texted Andrew to let him know she had decided to begin writing mysteries.

But Rosie's earlier comment about her lack of writing nagged at her, so Betsy erased what she'd typed and wrote, "I injured myself yesterday. The good news is – it wasn't any of my fingers."

Betsy finished the text when Detective Wilds drove in. He parked in his usual spot and exited his vehicle. His long strides towards them made it clear to those watching he had an agenda to accomplish.

He approached their campsite. "Ms. McCloud, I'll cut to the chase. Do you recognize this?" He produced a bag out of his jacket pocket. It held a half-inch thick pad of bright yellow paper.

Dillon sprang from her chair and grabbed the possible evidence from the detective's hand. "Isn't this the paper the notes were written on?"

"It needs more analysis, but we suspect it is. However, pages are missing. And there are indentations where someone wrote on the pad."

"Good work, Officer. But unless fingerprints show up on it, we're back to the beginning. No physical body. No crime." Dillon held the bag in the air. "Can I open it to examine it closer?" A resounding humph, and a slew of mumblings spewed from his lips. And, to accentuate his apparent frustration, he slapped a pair of gloves into the author's palm. She slipped them on and took the pad out of the bag.

"I didn't hear what you said. Repeat it for all of us to hear."

"Ms. McCloud, I said it would be easier if you didn't know so much about forensics."

"Our presence may irritate you, but without us – you wouldn't have some of the evidence."

"Dillon's right, and furthermore, your mama must have missed the lesson on teaching you to enunciate your words?"

"Mrs. Wilford, my mother taught me a little bit of everything, especially speaking clearly. She was one of the first female officers in St. Augustine. My siblings and I learned how to behave, or we'd know what day of the week it was."

"Good to hear." Dillon returned the sealed bag to the officer. "Can we get back to this pad of paper? Where does this lead us? Will it help us find the body? And do we have to stay here while we wait for more evidence to show up?"

Betsy hobbled over to her friend. "Snarkiness is never the answer, but a Rosie-inspected-and-approved hug is. Detective Wilds, you're the first." Bets hugged him, and it appeared he didn't know what to make of it. "Dillon, you're next."

The mystery writer smiled and said, "Bring it on."

"You go, Girlfriend." Rosie wore a Texas-size grin on her face. "I've taught you well. Now let's pray the Lord leads us to find the DB."

"DB?" Betsy, Dillon, and the detective said it at the same time.

"DB is slang for 'dead body.' I Googled crime scenes while Betsy hugged everyone. Somebody has to do some work around here. And I'm getting it done. Now it's time to pray. Heavenly Father, oh wait, I have a question for Officer Wilds – are you a Christian?"

"I am."

"If you'd said no, we'd have had a Come to Jesus meeting right here at the campground. Now let's pray. Bow your head."

Betsy couldn't tell for sure, but Rosie's voice may have fluttered the fronds on the palm trees with her zealous prayer. Indeed, the Lord heard her pleas, along with everyone else in the campground. As a result, a revival meeting took place at their site.

"And, thank You, Lord, for bringing to this old woman's attention what I found today. In Jesus' Name. AMEN!!!"

Everyone stared at Rose after her comment, and Bets saw her squirming under the scrutiny. She finally said, "Okay, already. This white piece of paper fell out of the compartment when I got out the chairs. I thought it was a receipt, but there's a number written on it."

"So you touched it?" The detective pushed his lower lip with his index finger, holding it there for an extended period of time. He then released it and said, "Can you give me whatever you found?"

Rose dangled the piece of paper in front of her, and as it dropped into his hand, she asked, "Am I going to jail?"

"I'm not arresting you, but can one of you turn on the light on your phone so I can examine this? The writing is too faint to make out." He held it close to his face.

I don't want to ask, but where is his cellphone or flashlight? Despite her silent question, all three of the ladies turned on their lights. Betsy laughed at the sight, causing her beam to bounce around. Rosie elbowed her, and she straightened up.

"It is a phone number and a couple of squiggly lines. Dillon, do you recognize any of it?" Wilds showed it to her.

"I better. It's my phone number. The rest. I'm not sure what it means."

~~~

The detective deposited the note in a separate bag and started to walk away but stopped. "Hang out at the campground for another day, and I'll remind you once again – don't do anymore snooping. Promise?"

They gave him an affirmative nod, which must have satisfied him because he walked away. Betsy watched his exit after she returned to her comfy lawn chair. *Sir, we're not ones to renege on a promise, but we'll be ferreting around the campground at the first ray of sunshine tomorrow.*

Rose set off in the direction of the office while Dillon lit the kindling in the fire pit. Another niggling feeling cartwheeled in Betsy's gut—this time about the latest note. Why wasn't she able to find it in the compartment? *Oh, a chair falling on my foot interrupted me.*

A little while later, Rosie reappeared with marshmallows and whatever else she'd found to purchase. "Betsy Stevenson, you're giving me the uglies, but don't you worry. I've bought healthy snacks this time too."

"Moon pies are not on the food pyramid."

"But baby carrots are. No more S'mores or fast food

for me. From now on. I'm turning over a new leaf."

"Did Detective Wilds scare you so bad you've lost your appetite…and your senses?"

"Until I found the piece of paper, I wasn't part of the investigation. But now I've touched evidence someone tucked in the folds of the umbrella inside my RV's compartment. The thought makes me shiver. The gall of someone. Brazen."

"Welcome to the world of crime and punishment." Dillon opened the bag of carrots and took a handful.

"That's what bugs me. The detective is going to get tired of hearing from us, but I may have another piece of the puzzle. Let's call him, and be sure to put it on speaker so all of us can listen to his response.

Dillon called, and as usual, he answered on the first ring. "Detective, Betsy has something to tell you."

"Go ahead."

"Before we took off for Savannah, Rose and Dillon left me alone in the RV. That's when I heard a sound like someone shut one of the outside compartments. I wondered at the time, but I attributed it to the wind. Or my imagination. It's obvious a person lifted the door and left his calling card."

"Thank you for telling me, Mrs. Stevenson. Talk to you soon."

~~~

Betsy's foot ached as she shifted positions on the couch. The uneasy feeling from earlier returned and kept her mind churning. *If someone opened and closed the compartment, wouldn't there be fingerprints on the door? And another opportunity the detective missed. Hmm.*

She clicked on the weather to see the forecast for the

next couple of days. Sunshine and blue skies with the usual humidity thrown in for Florida. Nothing to wash the evidence off the RV. "I am turning into a gumshoe, and I like it."

"And I'd like it if you hushed."

Betsy tucked under the covers and clicked her phone on again. The light blinded her, but when she could see, still no text from Andrew Pickle. He had said he'd be busy at three more writer's conferences in the next week or two after leaving Daytona.

And with Dillon's vlog every other day, he knew of their goings-on, but he'd never gone this long without contacting her. Guess she'd hear from him in a couple of days, or she'd keep texting him until he screamed, "I give."

Betsy changed positions and elevated her injured foot on a pillow. It helped the throbbing. She hoped the Tylenol would kick in, and sleep squelched her imagination running to and fro at 2:30 a.m.

Until then, she'd lie there and pray for whoever popped into her head. No surprise when the first person happened to be Detective Wilds.

~~~

The next morning, Betsy mentioned her concerns from the previous night about the compartment doors. "Dillon, please don't take offense but were you sleeping when Wilds said, 'Thanks. I'll talk to you soon.' Why didn't he dust for fingerprints on the RV yesterday, then send the results to the lab?"

"I have no idea, but I have a fingerprint kit at home. Wished I'd brought it, but who would have ever thought I'd have a use for it."

Rose munched on a banana while Dillon talked about

her forgetfulness. Betsy noted her friend's cheeks puffed out more with each bite. She finally asked her, "Are you going to swallow the monkey food, or are we going to wear the mushed-up fruit when you spit it out?"

She swallowed then gulped a drink of water. "I'm better, and please bear with me for what I'm about to suggest. It's a bit unlawful, but let me explain. And, if I do say so myself, it's the most brilliant plan I've manufactured in a long time." Rose pumped her fist.

"If it leans towards me spending time in jail, I'm not participating." Betsy stood and pointed to the boot. "I can outrun you with this on, and I will have the detective on the line before you can move."

"Dillon?"

"I have two good legs, Rosie, so you don't have a prayer. But please tell me what your *plan* is. It'll be interesting, like you."

"One of us has a compact with a cosmetic brush. It's thicker and perfect for Dillon to work her magic with the powder we place on the alleged fingerprint on the door of the compartment."

"You are proposing the most ridiculous—"

"There's more."

"I'm not surprised. Bets, how do you live with her every day? It has to be…" Dillon left her sentence unfinished and giggled.

"You laugh, but the second part diminishes our chance of spending a night or nights in jail. We do what Wilds showed us the other day. When a print shows up, we'll put packing tape over the evidence and take it to the police station. See, I thought of everything."

"While you were digging our perspective graves, I found the three closest police stations to us. Which one do you want?" Betsy showed them her phone. "Rosebud, however, you're looking at this – it is still illegal."

"I have the answer." Rose tapped her finger on her top lip as if in deep thought.

"To what, and are you going to tell us today?"

"This has nothing to do with fingerprints, but recently my matchmaking skills have noticed our detective has his eyes set on Dillon. He may be our man, and it's why he's delaying everything. Wilds wants to spend more time with her and—"

The author's phone rang. "Hello, Officer. As my mother used to say, 'Your ears must have been burning 'cause we were talking about you.'"

"I hope it's about me heading to check for fingerprints on Mrs. Wilford's outside compartment. I'm puzzled as to why you let me leave without doing it last night."

Betsy sprang off the couch with her booted foot and put a hand over Rose and Dillon's mouths. Both sputtered, and their eyes widened, but neither said anything.

"Ms. McCloud, are you there?"

"Detective, she's here, but can we call you back? It appears we've lost communication." She made a crackling noise into the phone and clicked it off.

"Do you want me to time his arrival, or are you going to do it, Dillon?"

"I'll do it, and I suggest we hide out in the office. We can talk while we watch the detective from the window."

They grabbed their phones and made a quicker trip to the office than Betsy's foot liked. Florence stood behind the counter. "Hello. Are you here for coff—"

"Don't mind us. We'll be right here by the window, shopping, shopping, shopping."

"Rose, my hand is itching to cover your mouth again. Shush." Betsy's whispered words made their mark, and her friend nipped it.

"I hope he does the job and leaves. If he does, we're bound for Fort Myers." Dillon kept her voice down. "He is going to have to travel to where we are. I'm not waiting for him or the nut's next move. Whoever it is."

"Whoever it is, they've already gone to great lengths to scare you, and they're aware of our plans to travel to southwest Florida."

"Bets, I'm counting on someone following us to Fort Myers. I have to find out who it is and let—"

"Ladies, warm muffins are sitting next to the coffee. They're free for the taking. And lookie here, Detective Wilds is heading this way."

"Is there another way out of here?" Dillon asked as she ran up to the counter.

"Why do you want anoth—"

"Help us."

Florence stretched her neck in the direction of the cooler. Betsy clutched her friends' arms, and they made it to the side door. Dillon opened it. "So, are you two with me, or do I have to Uber to Fort Myers?"

Betsy and Rose dashed/limped to the camper with Dillon in the lead. Thankfully, their spot sat close to the office. Bets caught her breath when they reached the RV, and Rose, between gasping for her own, said, "You two, go in and secure everything inside. I'll go unhook."

Pillows, blankets, and computers landed on the rear bed, shower door secured, and Dillon and Betsy buckled in. They waited for Rose. A short time later, she climbed into the driver's seat. "On the road again."

No one voiced their opinion on their quicker-than-normal departure out of the Restorative Cabins and Campground. Betsy settled in on the couch. Her thoughts on whether they'd left anything of importance behind, other than Detective Wilds.

~~~

"Ladies, I'm sorry for getting you into this mess. And, please don't hurt me, but I have a confession to make."

"Dillon, hold that thought until you put the Fort Myers Hobby Lobby in GPS. If you're wondering – we don't live at the craft store, but I can get us home from there. Okay, I'll shut up, and you can talk."

The author remained silent as she worked on Rose's request. Betsy's mind spun in all kinds of directions. *#1: Why are we evading police? #2: We can now classify ourselves as criminally insane. And #3: What else does Dillon have to spill? Things can't get much worse.*

"The directions are set, Rose. I've changed our itinerary, in case someone decided to follow us. Instead of I-95, we're taking I-4. You're less than twenty miles from it. Then it's clear sailing to the outskirts of Orlando and beyond."

Betsy waited for Dillon to elaborate, but the mystery writer sat back in her seat and stared out the window. So much for hearing about the confession she had eluded too. She'd leave it up to Rosie to ask her.

Bets relaxed on the couch, and her mind returned to the situation they'd put themselves in. For whatever reason, she found it amusing. The image of two older women and a thirty-something running from the authorities conjured up a comical image.

Any author would hope to write a scene like the one unfolding. No one could make this stuff up. And even if none of this matched what Betsy wrote, she'd somehow include it in her next book.

Betsy checked her phone one more time. Still no text or email from her editor. She determined she'd entered a rabbit hole that seemed to never end. And it hit her. *What if Dillon's confession was a setup for her newest book. And she'd played Rosie and her?*

Rosie's sudden acceleration and her jabbering brought Betsy out of her scattered thoughts. The words tumbling out of her friend's mouth came so fast, Dillon finally said, "Repeat and make it slower this time. But keep your eyes on what's ahead."

"We're…on…the…oh…my…a…confess…I…oh…"

"Dillon, she said, 'We're on the run, and she threw in an "oh my," and what's your confession. This is from me – and it better not include other law enforcement agencies." Betsy shook at the possibility of flashing lights and sirens surrounding the RV on a major thoroughfare.

"My confession has nothing to do with the police, which should put your minds at ease. So quit worrying about Detective Wilds. He's…"

Rosie's slight twitch with the steering wheel stopped Dillon's admission. And Betsy hollered from the couch. "I can drive, you know."

"Stay seated. I'm handling it."

"Good to hear. And this next statement is going to kill me, but this kind of conversation needs to take place when we're sitting still."

"To our next pit stop."

Dillon's words prompted Betsy to include, "It's hard to believe, but this morning we woke up as law-abiding citizens, but now we're outlaws. And, the driver will

adhere to what the speed limit signs tell her, won't she?"
"She will."

IT'S A MYSTERY...BIRDS

CHAPTER SEVEN

The miles melted away as Betsy peered out the side window. The landscape in the middle of Florida changed from marshland to farmland. The kind of vegetation stumped Bets. She'd missed Vegetable 101 in school, so if she spied a field in full bloom, she called it all sorghum.

Orlando had grown so much from the last time she and Ben visited Walt Disney World. City after city after city surrounded the tourist mecca. Kissimmee, once a sleepy town, had featured Busch Gardens. Their brochure drew them to the area.

So many years ago and buckets full of memories with her hubby. And lots more to come, but first, she had to let him know they'd changed their plans. No use mincing words. Blurt it out in a text. "Ben, we've hit the highway. We'll see you and the gang by dinner time."

She held her phone, and within seconds, it buzzed. "You're what?"

Her return text. "Calm down. I'll explain when we land. Can't wait to hug you." Betsy used a dozen emojis to express her mood. He answered with his own, and they covered four lines. On her next one, she added, "You are a hoot, Ben Stevenson."

"Anyone ready for a stop? My shoulder blades are screaming, and my hands ache from gripping the steering wheel. Glad we started a little later and missed rush hour."

"It's okay with me." Betsy marveled how Rosie referred to their getaway as "we started a little later." *No, my friend, we left the detective, spitting dust from our speedy departure. We are on the run.*

"Ladies, I Googled Sebring. It has tons of lakes." Dillon showed them her phone. "And for food - we have Mexican and Dee's Place. Oh, wait, this one will be Rosie's pick – Cowpoke's Watering Hole."

"The name alone has my vote. Cowpoke's it is."

Dillon touched the front of her phone, and directions to turn right in three hundred feet chimed out of it. She held it for Rosie to see, but it started to ring. She took her time turning it around, but in a swift swoop, she clicked it off.

Betsy saw the familiar name as it disappeared. "You'll have to answer his calls someday."

"Not today."

She left the subject alone and watched Rosie make the designated turns to the restaurant. As they had found in Savannah, parking an RV sometimes held more questions than answers, but today the back lot showed plenty of parking.

"You two go ahead. I'll be along in a minute."

Rose handled Dillon her keyring. "It's this one, and it fits in the top slot."

"Thanks. I'll see you in a few."

Bets opened the door, and the heat and humidity hit

her square in the face. "How about we change our plans…again…and go to Colorado?"

"Nope. We're almost home. And the faster we walk to Cowpoke's and eat, the quicker the tires will get rolling again.

On their stroll to the eatery, Betsy's fantasy of visiting her favorite state disappeared. Instead, worry replaced it as she speculated why Dillon stayed behind. Was she formulating a getaway plan so she didn't have to divulge her secret? "Nah. She'd find a rental, but nothing else."

"A rental for what, and who's renting it?" Rosie asked as she opened the door to the restaurant.

Their arrival nudged Betsy to pay attention, and she asked, "What are your thoughts on Dillon? She, along with us, escaped once. Maybe she'll try it again. Alone. Sebring, Florida isn't a place she'd find a Lyft or Uber to take her where she wants to go."

"How many in your party?" A hostess came forward with a tray full of water.

"Three. And we'll take three of those waters. Can we have a table? My legs are too short to reach the floor in a booth."

The young woman pointed to a four-topper. "Does this one work?"

"It does."

"I'll send your waitress with the water."

"Rosie, the hostess is aware you're short. TMI." Bets collected a menu stuck behind the napkins. While she perused it, delicious smells from the kitchen awakened her taste buds. Her eyes stopped at The Cowpoke's Big BLT. *Yummers.*

"Fish tacos sound delicious."

Betsy laid her menu on the table and started to ask

Rosie about her meal choice, but it stayed on the tip of her tongue when Dillon joined them. In a hurried tone, she said, "Can we get this to go?"

"Yes, you can get anything on the menu to go. What will you have?" The waitress tapped the order pad. "And, your meals are on the house. A gentleman paid for them—"

"You'll have to excuse me." Dillon sprang from her chair, causing it to topple, and sprinted out the door.

"She's not going to find him. He slipped an envelope to the hostess, giving her specific instructions for his money to go to Table #6."

"Were we already seated?" Rosie's voice trembled.

"You were. And from the stash Shelly said he gave her, the three of you can order anything you want."

"Can you ask her to come over here? We'd like to talk to her." Betsy hoped Dillon would return, but the author had planted herself next to Winnie B out in the parking lot. "Rosie, I'll be right back."

Bets strolled across the black-top parking lot, and when she reached her friend, she stated the obvious. "It's a tad warm out here to watch for someone who is long gone. Come back inside. The hostess may have a clue for us as to who he is."

Dillon led the way into the restaurant, and as they approached the table, she burst out with, "I hope she's not going to tell us the man wore a Speedo on his head and carried a piccolo?"

Any concerns Betsy had about her friend's state of mind dissolved at that moment. *She jokes at inappropriate times like I do. Thank You, Lord. I'm not alone.* And to celebrate, she signaled their waitress. "Since we're not drinkers, give us three malts in your to-go cups."

"Coming right up." The waitress strolled behind the counter.

A minute later, the hostess came to the table. "Hi. My name is Shelly. How can I help you?"

Dillon explained to the hostess what had occurred in St. Augustine without giving out too many details. "Shelly, I don't know why someone bought our lunch, but I'm curious, what did this man have on?"

"A Hawaiian shirt, shorts, and flip-flops."

"I hate to say it, but this man's ensemble broadens our search to include almost every male in the whole state of Florida," Rosie countered.

"Was there anything else abnormal about the man?" Dillon stood and made a gesture above her head. "How tall was he? I'm five feet ten inches. Was he taller than me?"

"Maybe an inch or two taller." Shelly stuck her nose in the air. "I do remember a smell when I seated him and when he handed me the money. Mr. Random Acts of Kindness smelled like the dump."

"The dump?" Rosie's voiced raised. "Does Sebring have a dump nearby?"

"It's off of Arbuckle Creek Road." Annabelle brought three malts to the table. "I can take your order when you're ready."

"We are. The BLT and fries will do it for me. Rosie wants fish tacos, and I don't know why. Dillon?"

"Hard to talk about food after discussing dumps, but give me a cheeseburger and onion rings."

"I'll put a rush on your order."

"Back to visiting the dump—I'm not going. No way. No how. And about accusing Mr. Stinky of committing the crime, or even deliberating on him, certifies we've all gone half cuckoo." Rose sipped on one of the malts. "Yum! Chocolate."

"I'm with Rosie. There is no possible way this person tailed us through the traffic we ran into in Orlando and beyond. It is too coincidental. And the logistics make it impossible. And I repeat – not every incident has to point to the case."

"Random acts of kindness happen to other people, not me. And when someone paid for our meal in the middle of all this today – it tends to creep me out. Bear with me. I'm past my threshold of handling anything. I'm officially giving it to the Lord."

Annabelle placed the bag of food next to the drinks. "I am sorry you won't be staying to eat. But, next time you visit Sebring, don't be in such a hurry. And, if you wouldn't mind, Ms. McCloud, can I get your autograph? I love your books."

Dillon's eyes brightened. "You're sweet. Do you have a book or a napkin for me to sign?"

"My apron. It will show people I met a celebrity. And I have a permanent marker for your signature."

Annabelle removed it, and Dillon signed above the ruffled edge and handed the pen to Betsy. "She's a famous author too. Check her out. Oh, and Rosie, she's famous for her hugs and her driving ability."

"Yes, you two ladies sign it too. I may have to frame this one and hang it on the wall. It's been a pleasure serving you."

Betsy took her turn then handed the marker to Rose, who commandeered the apron and the table to do her signature. Curly Qs filled the light blue waistband from one end to the other. "Do you have any other colors of pens?"

"Give her the pen. We're out of here. Thanks for your help. Both of you." Bets took the bag. "Time to eat."

~~~

They found a park next to a lake a mile down the road and sat at a picnic table under the shade of a live oak tree. Rosie opened her to-go box. "Dillon, I can eat while you tell us your secret. If you assumed I'd forgotten what you said, you're sadly mistaken."

"You're talking about my reference to a confession – right?"

Betsy tore the plastic off of her cutlery. "And I'm wondering why you stayed back in the RV at the restaurant. If our travels have proven anything – anything can and will materialize with the Early Birds, plus one. Remember, we're in this together."

"Bets, she's not a plus one. If you recall, Dillon asked to join the Early Birds the other day, and we spaced it. Today I'm making her an honorary member. If she chooses to accept the offer?"

"I do."

"Now, Ms. McCloud, confess away…on everything."

"My confession: Daytona or St. Augustine isn't where the mystery started. Please don't ask me what possessed me not to tell the detective this piece of information, but honestly, I'm doubting his credentials." The mystery writer took a drink of her malt.

Choking began, and Betsy's face changed three or four shades of red. Rose rushed to the side compartment and snatched three bottles of water. "Drink up. I want to hear this without interruptions."

"FYI: My gagging had nothing to do with Dillon's words. This Cowboy BLT has a kick. Sorry. Continue with your story."

"The notes started before Daytona. And, they were all written on the same paper found at the campground. The weirdest deal - a yellow rose appeared in my room at the conference. The front desk clerk said, 'We found it on the counter after lunch and delivered it to the name on the card.'"

"Did this person check surveillance? It may have been your boyfriend, wanting to surprise you."

"By the time I asked the hotel, Bets, they'd erased the tapes. No help there. And about Thomas, he's on assignment. No communication for the last three months, except for the other day when his friend called to check on me. He and his wife keep up on my vlog."

"Maybe this gentleman you spoke with ordered the flower for your boyfriend and had them delivered?" Rosie lowered her sunglasses. "But the most important question is – what did the card say?"

"I'd be surprised if it came from Thomas. He's not the romantic type. And the card said, 'Forgiveness mends a broken heart.' Great saying, but is it telling me the person forgives me, or I'm supposed to forgive them?"

"Whichever way, it's advice we all should heed." Rose picked up her taco, but then said, "Dillon, I know you doubt the detective, but I am surprised you kept this from him."

"On top of what Rosie said, we ran out on him. If he's legit or not, Wilds is a rather large man who carries a badge and a gun. Handcuffs don't go with this outfit."

"Betsy, I'm certain none of us will be wearing handcuffs, but I have more to tell you. While you two strolled into the restaurant, I made a call to the campground. I asked to speak to Florence. Are you ready for this? They don't have anyone working there with that name."

"What?" Rose and Betsy rang in at the same time. Then Bets added, "What about ukulele man?"

"I didn't ask about Mark or whatever his name was. Why don't you give them a call to see if they've heard of the maintenance man?"

"I'll call them right now and—." A boat on the lake revving its motor silenced additional words, so Betsy hobbled away from the table to hear her phone. The noise subsided, and the campground answered.

She plowed ahead, "Hi, I'm Betsy Stevenson, and my friends and I stayed at your place last night."

"Yes, hi. You were one of the ladies traveling with Dillon McCloud?"

"Uh huh. And why I'm calling is I'd like to talk to Mark. Is he still around?"

Betsy heard a rustling sound on the other end of the phone then silence. She presumed she'd lost the connection, but the woman said, "He's gone home for the day. Can I leave him a message? He'll be in at 9:00 in the morning."

After giving the woman her phone number, she said, "I don't recognize your voice. Were you at the campground while we were there?" The background noise started again, but this time the connection dropped, leaving Betsy holding a dead phone. "Houston, we have a problem."

~~~

They piled into Winnie B, and Betsy called Ben as Rose pulled into the gas station. "Hon, get Larry. He needs to hear this too. As I said earlier, we're heading to Fort Myers, and we'll be home soon, but I'm giving you a warning. What I'm about to tell you isn't a joke."

"What do you mean?"

"Larry and Ben, we're up to our neck in trouble—maybe—sort of. And it has to do with us dodging the detective this morning. Another important tidbit is we think he or the person who played dead at the campground is chasing us."

"Is that all?" Betsy's hubby chuckled.

"This isn't funny, Mr. Stevenson. Your wife is not exaggerating. We're in trouble clear up to our painted-on eyebrows. And it's why we're not laughing. You two better pull it together by the time we get into town."

"Rose, we'll do our best, but can you blame us for finding humor in this? I'm speaking for your husband now, but when you and my wife are involved – mayhem of cosmic proportions tends to occur. Please put Ms. McCloud on. She has to verify what you've said."

"Here she is."

"Dillon, is my wife making this up? It sounds pretty farfetched. We know the part about the disappearing body, but all of you being on the lamb? Are you kidding with us?"

"It's the truth. We fled out the side door of the office, and we're in Sebring, Florida now. What they've said is true."

"What have you done with our wives? They'd rather put toothpicks unde—" Laughter erupted on the other end of the phone.

"Glad you two are finding such humor in our peril. We'll trade places with you anytime." Betsy attempted to keep the indignation out of her voice, but she failed.

"We're sorry. Hon, it's not your norm to break the law."

"You think." Betsy's head and foot throbbed, and she didn't know which hurt worse. "All I know, Ben, it is getting stranger by the minute. And now I have a headache to add to my foot pain. Anyway, we have to get gas or get out of the way. We'll talk to you in a while. Bye."

"Can't wait to hear more of your saga."

"I'm with him."

While Dillon and Rose scurried out of their doors, Betsy ended her call and noticed them from her perch at the table. The older of the two wanted to pay for the gas, but the mystery writer – with her card in hand – ran it and captured the nozzle.

"Lord, are You watching this nonsense?" Bets glanced out at her friends again as Rosie grabbed the window squeegee from Dillon. Water dripped on both of their feet. "Oh, how I wish all of this was behind us, and we were on our way to Ashe—"

"Asheville?" Dillon stood at the screen door. "Did we make a wrong turn?"

"Nope. We're still heading southwest. And before you ask, you heard me having a conversation with the Lord. He's an excellent listener. Other days, you might catch me talking to myself. Either way, it helps to pass the time."

"All the authors I'm associated with chat with themselves. But when it comes to brainstorming, I go straight to the Lord. And I let Him do all the talking. It's had amazing results."

"That's encouraging to hear, and I definitely need to do more listening. And to the subject of our driver – what is taking Rosie so long?" Betsy checked outside for the third time. "Oh, I see her. She's coming, and she's bringing a person with her."

Rosie came up to the door. "Betsy, come on out. And Dillon, you stay put. Your biggest fan wants to meet you. I may have dropped your name while I stood at the soda fountain, and the next thing I know—the fizz off of this woman's drink is running down my cheek. God bless you, Alice."

Betsy wanted no part of the party outside but noticed Dillon's slower than normal steps shouted apprehension. *Why is Rosie bringing a stranger over here? What does this woman want? Is it an autograph, or is she following us?*

"Earth calling Betsy. Are you staying inside or what?" Rose's voice penetrated her deep and menacing thoughts.

"I'm on my way."

As Betsy made it out the door, the woman said, "Dillon, I've read all of your books, and I adore your vlog." The woman blushed. "I'm not stalking you, but when you hinted at your location yesterday, I prayed to catch a glimpse of you."

Plausible, but not probable. Huh! But one issue - she's not mentioned specific locales in any of her vlogs. "Ladies, I don't want to be a dampener of delight for Alice meeting her beloved author, but we have a schedule to keep. So, Rosie, get your hugs, and we're off."

During Rose's hugfest, Betsy kept an eye on Alice. After their goodbyes, the woman rushed away. Bets scurried Dillon and Rose into the RV and slammed the door. "FYI: We're moving to the parking lot next door to people watch. See if anyone tries to follow us."

"You're scaring me. There is nothing wrong with

Alice. And, again I say, we cannot be leery of everyone we meet." Rose started the RV. "Me and the Lord aren't one pinch worried about His people. Unlike someone else in this RV."

As her friend drove to the shoppette and parked, Betsy peered at Alice from the side window. The pesky headache she'd complained about to her hubby – a mere memory because her heightened sense of sniffing out a possible suspect took over her brain waves.

For a second, she lost sight of Alice, so she moved to the back window. She caught their new acquaintance as she jumped into the passenger side of a vehicle. The car pulled out of the gas station, and none other than Florence from the campground occupied the driver's seat.

"Rosebud, I've changed my mind. Floor it. Catch that silver sedan. When it's possible, pass them, and you'll see what I'm talking about."

Again, Rose followed Betsy's directions and pulled in behind the car. Florence (or her twin) slowed, giving them an opportunity to get around them. When they were window to window, Bets hollered, "Dillon, look down at the driver. Should be of interest to you."

They cleared the vehicle, and Dillon yelled, "We're being tailed. And I'm going to find out why. Rose, put your flashers on and ease off the road. My guess, they'll speed past us. When they do, get Winnie B back on the road, and we'll chase after them…wherever they go."

"Ooh. A chase scene right out of the movies. Hold on. We'll corner them like a cat going after a mouse." She put on her turn signal and slowed onto the shoulder.

"Sometimes, Mrs. Wilford, you can make sense. And if all of us agree, I'm ready to play their game. I pray they'll show us what they're up to. Other than driving us crazy. Lord, be with us now!"

Rosie kept moving at a slow speed as she crept to the side of the road. The sedan sped past them, as Dillon predicted. As soon as traffic cleared, her friend hit the road in hot pursuit of the other vehicle.

"Great driving, but keep your distance. We don't want to spook the driver."

"My feathers remain unruffled, but they are stirring my pot a tiny bit."

If someone had told Betsy she'd compliment Rose on her display of calmness in this type of situation – she'd have said, "Not going to happen." Usually, her friend's emotions zigzagged between frenzied and flustered in most circumstances.

But not this time. "Rosie, keep doing what you're doing. And since Winnie B sits higher than their passenger car, I'll keep my eyes focused on their vehicle. It looks like the Lord has blessed us with less traffic today."

For some unknown reason, Rosie tooted the horn. "If any of you are wondering, the gas gauge is still showing full. I do hope they stop before they land in the Gulf of Mexico. I'm not into getting wet." A snort escaped.

"Rose, the getaw—"

"Away car has their turn signal on. I'm on it."

"Stay back. It may be a trick." Dillon leaned forward in her seat.

"They're taking the side road. I'm following them, even if they take us through the orange grove. And Lord, keep Winnie B together wherever we may travel."

Citrus trees lined both sides of the county road, and a quick survey of the rows between the trees revealed no recreational vehicle would fit through without tearing off the sides and top of it.

A car had a better chance, but even they would have to be stupid to attempt such a feat. Betsy saw them slowing down, and Florence made a quick turn into a small clearing. A dust cloud enveloped the RV.

"They're getting away."

"They're not if I can help it." Rose had reduced her speed to make the turn then accelerated. The gravel on the one-lane road caused quite a racket on the undercarriage of Winnie B. "Don't worry, she's built Ford Tough."

"This isn't the time for a commercial, but I'm thrilled she's not going to fall apart. I want to catch them." Betsy moved from the couch to the banquette, hoping to help her friends keep the fleeing vehicle in view.

Dillon held the expanded map of Florida for all to see. "The road has to stop somewhere. Either this leads to a house or a swamp. It's up for grabs as to which one at this point."

"The car stopped up ahead. See?" Rosie slowed and inched into a driveway. Once parked, she shot out of the RV and around the front of it…in time to collide with Dillon. They attempted to sidestep one another, but it ended in the same predicament.

Betsy finally yelled out the window. "Rosebud, stand still. Dillon, you go on ahead. This is your circus."

~~~

"Someone better spill it, or I'm calling the police."

"Ms. McCloud, you don't have to." Detective Wilds rolled the window down and stuck his head out.

Seeing the officer as he got out of the vehicle sent shivers down Betsy's spine, and she imagined he'd called the Lee County cops on their way through the orchard. She feared they'd come and put the three of them in the hoosegow. "I hope Ben knows I love him."

"I don't know what Bets is talking about, but you, Mister – what is this all about?" Rosie pointed in the direction of the car. "I recognize Florence and the other lady who claimed to be my friend back at the gas station. Who else is hiding in the back seat?"

"No one, but…but…" The detective stammered and waltzed to the back door of the car and opened it. "You may recognize my cousin."

A person righted herself and gasps from Betsy, Rose, and Dillon greeted her. "Hi Dillon, it's me."

"Arlene Peterson?" Dillon closed her eyes and rubbed her forehead. "All I can say is why?"

"It's me, and I guarantee you will find all of this quite amusing when I tell you about it. And—"

"And I wouldn't count on it." The mystery writer leaned against the RV. "Arlene, you have a whole lot of explaining to do. And your job of working for me is—I don't mean to use alliterations, but it is tipping towards termination."

"Let me explain." Arlene jumped out of the back seat and raced to Dillon. "We did it to help you get your writer's block unstuck." She turned to Betsy. "I bet it worked, and she's writing as she did years ago."

"I'm not saying your ploy worked, but she no longer needs to sleep. Her fingers fly across the keyboard every night. But, why pull a stunt of placing a pretend dead man in the laundry room?"

"We had nothing to do with the disappearing person. We only planted the notes, and with your background in forensics, you'd have to call in the cops. This is where my cousins, Detective Wilds and Florence, come in."

Cousins? Betsy's mouth dropped close to a foot, and the latest newsflash caused it. But even with this newest development, Betsy wondered if they'd still have to spend time behind bars. *But, if there's not a body?*

As if he'd read her mind, the detective said, "Ladies, you're not off the hook just yet." Wilds stood next to Arlene. "I came to the campground this morning to release you to continue your travels, but you left without my authorization. And, by the way, the case is still active."

"I'm curious. If the supposed crime happened in St. Augustine, what are you doing following us to Lee County?"

"I take the blame for us tailing you. But, the tracker—" Arlene's hand covered her mouth.

"And tracking you through the backcountry of Florida hasn't been easy," the detective interjected.

Everyone's attention turned to Wilds, and Betsy lost interest in a possible jail sentence when he admitted he and Arlene had committed their own crime. *If I weren't so pudgy, I'd crawl under Winnie B and hunt for the tracking device. Now it makes total sense.*

Rosie's eyes lit up. "I have an idea. We've come this far with everyone." She hooked her arm into the detective's. "How about we go all the way to Fort Myers? I want to hear more of this story."

"No one is coming with us anywhere, Rose, except for you, me, and Betsy. And I've heard enough." Dillon walked a few steps then pivoted to face Arlene. "I do have to say a tracking device is clever, but it's also illegal."

"But, Dillon, let me explain. There's more. So much

mo—."

"Move away from her. The three of you heard Dillon. Head 'em out in the opposite direction." Rose's arm movements directed them to the road as if the occupants of the sedan had forgotten.

"Enough already, Rosie." Betsy hobbled to the RV where Dillon now sat. As for her other friend, she lagged behind. Bets hoped the group left, and they'd not have to contend with them again. *But what if they continue to keep track of us somehow?*

Bets propped her foot on the banquette, and the sniffling sound from the front seat prompted her to ask, "Dillon, you go ahead and cry. It'll make you feel better."

"I'm not sure it will. Finding out most of what happened was a prank aggravates me. I appreciate Arlene's concern for my writing, but the trickery doesn't sit well with me. I'm done with it all."

"Don't say another word." Betsy opened the door and yelled. "Mrs. Wilford, get your hindquarters in here now."

"I'll be right there."

"Not good enough." Betsy limped to the sedan and let loose on anyone within earshot. "Whatever Rose has conveyed to you. Ignore it. Take your tracking device and point your car in the direction we're not going. There…will…be…no…following…us. Do you understand?"

Heads nodded, and the ladies scattered. Wilds climbed under the RV, and in seconds, he held the device. "Found it." He dusted off his pants on his way to the idling vehicle. As he attempted to close the door, Florence peeled out and left dust in her wake. Again.

"Since they're gone, let's get out of here. I sense alligators lurking, and they're adding us to their dinner menu." Betsy led Rose to the driver's side and stopped. "And now that we have answers to part of the mystery, we can enjoy some downtime when we get to Fort Myers."

"Aren't either of you curious about the rest of their story?" Rose placed her hand on the door handle.

"No, and Rosie, neither are you. If the Lord wants to fill us in on the details, He will figure out a way to tell us. It's none of our business. And when we get inside Winnie B, let's leave Dillon alone. She's had enough excitement for one day."

She'd toned down her last two sentences, but when the driver's window came down, Betsy guessed Dillon had heard their conversation when she said, "After we land in Fort Myers, drop me at the Lighthouse Resort. I have a reservation. The excitement has caught up with me."

Rosie opened her mouth to speak, but Betsy interrupted her, "Great idea. You can sit in the hot tub and let all your troubles melt away."

~~~

After they landed at their RV Park, Betsy exited and hugged her husband tight around the neck. "Ben Stevenson, I am so glad to be home. This last week felt as if it lasted a month. It'll be wonderful to sleep in my bed tonight."

"Hon, I missed you too." He gave her a quick smooch. "Larry, you better inspect your rig. After the stories our wives shared with us, a new one may be in your future."

"We haven't imparted the latest one yet." Again, Betsy opened the side compartment, this time not worried about fingerprints or notes falling out, and retrieved four chairs. "This one will take a while."

As Ben took his seat and hooked Matilda's leash next to him, he asked, "Did you lose Dillon on your way to Fort Myers?"

"She's at the Lighthouse Resort, and she promised she'd come over tomorrow. Now about our travels home. I've uttered these words on other occasions, but they're apropos again. What you're about to hear will curl the hair you haven't grown yet."

The story of their return trip took Betsy, with Rosie's help, an hour to tell. The men interrupted them more than once. At one point, she wanted to stuff a sock into both of their mouths and finally said, "Sit and listen. We'll take questions after we're done."

Betsy's final statement, "Arlene revealed her part in the caper, but the other woman...she left us in the dark as to why she participated in the prank – other than being Arlene's cousin. She has a large family, and my gut tells me there's more to this story."

"If you would have let me invite them here, they'd have spilled their guts. And I've always said Dillon knows more than she's disclosing. But I'm a little bit curious where the detective fits in – she said he's her cousin but is he a real detective? What about Florence? Or the maintenance/ukulele man?"

"I'll be surprised if I hear from Mark, but he's supposed to call tomorrow. We can hope someone confesses. Without a confession, it's still a tangled web of who knows what. And it's time to say goodnight and go to our RVs. Come on, Matilda. It's treat time for all of us."

"Lar, I'm hankering for some ice cream. And Betsy,

let me know if you hear from the maintenance man." Rosie made her way inside her RV.

"You can count on it." Bets shut the door and leaned against it. "Ben, I'd appreciate this chapter, no pun intended, to be over. Tomorrow, I'll find out if the craziness will continue. Lord, please help us if it does."

IT'S A MYSTERY...BIRDS

CHAPTER EIGHT

Betsy made countless calls to the campground throughout the week, but the office gave her one excuse after another. Either he worked the late shift on a particular day, or he'd called in sick.

While she waited for a return call, Dillon came to see Sassy Seconds *Two*. She adored the concept of dressing those less fortunate for success in the workplace. By mid-week, she'd started to work at the second-hand store.

Today, however, Dillon had taken the day off to write, which made Betsy spend too much time on her foot, and it screamed at her. And she still waited for a call from Mark at the campground.

Bets limped away from Rose and lowered herself into a chair. Then her phone jingled. *Please let it be Ukulele Man.* A peek at her phone showed Potential Spam. Betsy shut it off and decided to give up on ever hearing from the maintenance man. "We're back to where we start—"

"I don't mean to interrupt you talking to yourself." Dillon stood in front of Betsy. "But you'll appreciate my news. I woke up at 3:30 this morning and started typing.

Words were pouring out of my fingers. I've found paradise. When my lease expires, I'm moving to Florida."

Bets straightened in her chair. "I thought you took the day off. And don't say this new development too loud. If the person we haven't located knows your whereabouts, he'll have your address programmed in his phone, and you haven't booked your moving truck yet."

Rose stared at them, and while she folded a tie-dyed t-shirt, she said, "Bets, this is the most ludicrous idea you've come up with so far. But right now, I need you to stick this on the shelf with the other wild-colored items?"

"Did you hear, Dillon? She said she's moving to the Sunshine State, and you're way too calm. Something's up."

"Nothing is up. I'm calm because the Lord has blessed us with this wonderful news. He's supplied more than enough worker bees, and the roof is repaired. And here comes my favorite employee, except you two. Everly, what's on your mind – other than your upcoming wedding?"

"We've had a change of plans." Everly breezed into the room. "The crew fixed our roof, but with the torrential rains last night, our reception venue called to say they had to close due to leaks in their roof."

"Sweetie, what are you going to do?"

"Douglas and I talked. Can we use this room? With black tablecloths and silver decorations, it will work."

In an instant, Rose's tranquil disposition became extinct. Chaotic dance moves replaced it. And, her voice carried throughout the warehouse when she uttered, "We'll have to rearrange the tables and hang the chandeliers from the women's store in here. Everly, any other ideas?"

"So is it a 'yes?'"

"It sure is. Larry Wilford, what are you doing? Put the hotdog down and come over here."

"We have plenty of time, Rose. Douglas is on a ladder, and he…"

Rosie's short legs carried her to the side door, but she stopped and planted her fists on her hips. "If our groom falls off of it again, Mr. Wilford, God's grace and mercy won't be enough to save your hide. Oh, Everly, come with me. We'll save your man from utter doom."

"Larry, you better go get him down. She'll end up hurting herself." Dillon shooed him away and returned to fold a t-shirt. "Oh, and if you sweet talk her, it works too."

"Or not." Larry smiled.

"It never hurts to try. But my advice to you, and for everyone's safekeeping, is to hire another person without an injured limb to climb up the ladder and do whatever job needs doing."

"Great advice, Bets. I'm on it." He tossed the last of his lunch in the trash and departed through the same door as his wife. A minute later, Betsy heard Larry say, "Rosebud, let go of his good leg and allow him to get off the ladder by himself."

Betsy chuckled. "You do come in when foolishness is at its peak. And you handle it so well, which is quite a chore. But back to your news – I'm happy the words are flowing again. And on top of writing, you're a big help at the store."

"I minored in fashion design in college and majored in journalism. I felt it was a wise decision to have something to fall back on if making a living as a writer peters out."

Betsy saw the door to Dillon's past spring open, and she jumped in with both feet. "Did you meet your boyfriend in one of your classes in college?"

"We met in one of my forensic classes our freshman year. He said, 'I'm taking this class to find out if you'll go out with me.'"

"What a pick-up line."

"I hate to admit it, but it was short-lived, but thanks to mutual friends, we hooked up again a couple of years later. And as with any relationship, we talked about marriage but then decided we liked it the way it was. We both love our freedom."

"Which makes it easy for you to hitch a ride in an RV with two strangers, who are a tad looney."

"Something along those lines."

Betsy glimpsed sadness in her friend's eyes and attempted to lighten the mood. "I can't imagine you'd want to miss out on wedded bliss you seen exhibited today. Did you know they're teaching a marriage class next week called: 'Love Abounds Amongst Threats of Bodily Harm'?"

"That's a class I'd attend, even if I'm not the marrying kind." The writer inhaled. "She hasn't actually..."

"Heavens no. Rose threatens but never carries through on them. But she does love to exaggerate, embellish and assemble stories with the best ending, which suits her...her preferred storyline, though, is playing matchmaker."

"I'm glad I haven't given her anything to work with in the romance department."

"Dillon, she does know about your boyfriend, so don't be surprised if he shows up unexpectedly from the far-reaches and proposes. I wouldn't put it past her. She's like an alligator on an egret."

"I'll be watching her. But, Betsy, I do have a little secret that I can share with you. Arlene is the only one who is privy to what I'm about to tell you. Another lifetime ago...I was engag—"

A crash in the other room stopped Dillon, and she ran out of the room. Betsy made her way to the commotion a bit later. Her heart quickened when she saw Rosie leaning over her husband. "Sweetums, speak to me. Please, Lord, help him to hold on until the EMTs arrive."

Larry sat up and rubbed the side of his leg. "I tripped over the ladder. And it fell before I could catch it. I'm not hurt. See?" He stood and moved around before he picked it up and propped it against the wall. He then limped away into the other room.

"You do carry on, Rose."

"You're right. Next time, Bets, I'll let him lie there, writhing in pain."

"No, you won't, but you better find out why Everly's expression appears as if she swallowed a carrot whole. Dillon and I are leaving you two to hang men's clothes. Come when you can." Betsy scooted her author friend to the other room. "You were saying?"

"I've changed my mind. It's not important."

"Ms. McCloud, I'm a new investigator on your case. Whatever is going on in your life – present or past – is important. Any detail may help solve the final piece of the puzzle. So spill your 'little' secret. I'll keep it sealed between these lips." Bets pointed at them. "Rosie will never find out."

"Rosie will never find out what?"

"Why are you not in helping Everly?" Betsy wanted

to throttle her friend for interrupting. Again. But she only held a man's suit jacket. At last count, not the deadliest of weapons.

"I'm listening. Oh, and Everly is fine. A piece of granola careened down the wrong pipe. A little water – and nothing is amiss any longer. Go ahead, Dillon, tell me what I'm not supposed to find out."

"About my wedding plans." The writer sighed and hung her head. When she looked up again, sadness had returned to her eyes. "I might as well tell both of you about the nuptials which didn't take place."

"I thought you had an aversion to marriage?" Bets questioned her friend.

Dillon's face resembled Everly's the minute before, and Betsy handed her a water bottle. She took a swallow and said, "I guess it's time I talk about it. My intended groom was An…Andrew…Pickle."

"Say what? My editor?"

"Honey, don't mind Betsy. Just tell us all about it, but first, clear up a loose end for me. I've heard you speak of Thomas, but you've never said a word about Andrew? He did seem to get on your nerves quite a lot at the conference."

Dillon sat down. "After Thomas and I broke up our freshman year, Andrew and I dated. We planned our future together. I'd write, and he'd grow his publishing company. Then something happened, and I chickened out and relocated to New York City."

She paused, giving Betsy time to spot the hurricane in the making across from her, i.e., Rose. Her mouth resembled a nutcracker general. It opened, but nothing emerged. Bets took the reins, "She wants to say she's sorry to hear the sad news. So am I."

"Betsy, thanks for answering for me. And I mean it sincerely. What I had romping around in my brain sounded judgmental – in all caps."

"I'd deserve it, Rose. But, as far as I'm concerned, marriage and writing cannot coexist. And it still can't."

"And this is why I think the Lord orchestrated your meeting and subsequent friendship with Betsy. She and Ben have quite the testimony, which ties right into your situation."

"Betsy, you married someone before Ben? Please don't tell me you left him at the alter?"

"Heavens no. What she's talking about is when I started to write books twenty-plus years into our marriage. We learned it doesn't work for couples to seek their own way." Betsy touched one of the floral ties. "Marriage is working together for a common goal."

"Marriage is whatever you make it, Bets. I'm glad yours worked out. But, it's too confining for me. Life is easier by myself. And, I'm out of here. Today I'm driving to the beach to see if there's a bungalow for rent. Hey, if the price is right – I may buy it."

Dillon left the warehouse, and Betsy resumed her task of hanging up the new arrivals. But Rosie's dance moves from the other side of the table prompted her to ask, "You must have news to tell me because you know where the bathrooms are."

"This is news you'll be interested in." Rose tapped her finger to her chin. "While we were at the conference, Andrew asked me about our travel plans. I told him we were heading to St. Augustine on Monday morning."

"Rosie, since Dillon and Andrew have a history, I don't find it strange he'd ask where we were headed. And I know where you're going with this – but him posing as the dead man? I doubt it." Betsy massaged the back of her neck. "It has to be the maintenance man."

"From the description Dillon gave the detective, he's too short."

"You're right." Betsy envisioned the man next to her in the shed, and he stood no more than five foot seven, at best.

"I thought it peculiar at the time, but now I'm wondering if Andrew isn't Dillon's creepy crawler. Bets, you have his number. We have some investigating and a tad bit of matchmaking to get done. Maybe they can be the second couple who gets hitched around here.

~~~

Betsy called her editor, and much to her surprise – he answered with, "I saw your text, but I dropped my phone in the sink later that day. I lost all my contact information. I'm glad you finally called me."

She considered his excuse, but it made little to no sense. He could have gotten on his computer to find her contact information. *Okay, buddy, I can play your game too.* "No worries, Andrew, we've been busy, busy, busy traveling around."

"I hope all of you are having a good time."

"We are, but I'm curious why you wanted to know what our plans were after the conference. Have you ventured to St. Augustine in the last two weeks? I'm asking this because unusual things happened while we camped there."

Betsy didn't want to give too much away, but when you're investigating a possible crime – you pulled out the clown suit if it'd solve the wrongdoings. "Andrew, I have one more question. Do you own a musical instrument?"

A long pause signaled he'd either hung up, or he rehearsed the story he'd tell her. Betsy tolerated a bit of silence but then said, "Spit it out. You are or aren't our suspect. Or is there another nut case on the loose? If the latter is the one, your ex-fiancé is in danger."

Another lengthy gap ensued. Betsy waited. Finally, when he spoke, Andrew said, "I borrowed the ukulele as a last-minute addition but returned it. The rest of the outfit was used to hide my identity. Betsy, I'm sorry I did it. She's never going to believe anything I say or do again."

"I'd say you *better* be sorry. And there's a detective in St. Augustine who is very interested in what you have to say. I'd suggest you call this number." Betsy gave it to him. "Start with an apology for taking up his time. Your next call will be to Dillon to explain your rationale."

"Son, this is Rose. For the time being, don't call Dillon. I believe a face-to-face meeting is in order to explain yourself. You need to get down here to Fort Myers ASAP and make amends with our author friend. The one you're still in love with."

"I have to agree with Rosie. But this time, come as Andrew Pickle. She'll be much more receptive to you without seeing underwear on your head, which to me was a little bizarre. Can't wait to hear your explanation about it when you get here."

"I'll see you tomorrow afternoon."

Betsy hung up and texted the store's address to Andrew. She then asked Rose, "What do we do first? Other than keeping our traps shut for one whole day. Rosebud, do you have the ability not to flap your chops to Dillon?"

"It won't be an issue. You'll see, but we have to get busy planning an intimate dinner for Dillon and Andrew. But I am concerned after the shock of seeing him and hearing his side of the story. You and I may have to intervene by strapping her to the chair."

Bets envisioned her writer friend wearing a straitjacket. "Constraints may hamper the sole purpose of a romantic evening, but we'll pray Dillon settles down and gives Andrew a chance to explain himself."

"I can feel another matchmaking success story in my bones."

"Rosie, we're forgetting an important part of the puzzle."

"What are you talking about?"

Rose's feigned surprise tickled Bets. "I'll refresh your memory. Thomas. Her boyfriend. Ring any bells?"

"I hear the ringing, but Dillon's face lit up when she talked about Andrew today. This fact has to rank higher than when she's said anything about Thomas. Do I have to mention he's not even in the U.S. of A. long enough to have breakfast, lunch, or dinner with her?"

"Good point, but he's still part of her life."

"He is, but your editor has to come clean and tell her how he feels. And, what an ideal place to tell her the truth than at a dinner made especially for the two of them? We'll set the stage. Whatever happens afterward is up to them."

"Where are we holding the dinner party at your RV or mine?"

"It may be a challenge, but we can have it here at the thrift shop. With Dillon gone, we have all afternoon to plan an unforgettable event. I'll text Lar to tell him we're spending the evening here."

"Leave out the part about us matchmaking, but ask Larry and Ben if they'll do us a favor and run to the store to pick up a prime rib. I don't want to stop decorating to have to do a grocery run."

"On it." Rose texted her husband, and while her fingers were still moving, she asked, "Anything else?"

"There is one more thing – you're cooking the meat. Remember, I don't like to cook."

"We're all aware of that. Thank goodness you learned how to make potato salad from your mom. It's the best. And I'm going into the next room and get a snack. All this talk of food made me hungry."

Rose's mention of a side dish prompted Betsy to call her hubby. When he answered, she said, "Ben, while you and Lar are at the store picking up the meat, grab two baking potatoes, a bag of salad, and a dessert you like. I'll explain later."

~~~

While their husband's shopped, Rose and Betsy, with Everly's help, began transforming one of the larger dressing rooms into a magical wonderland. The younger woman had located three bolts of chiffon in a light, dusty gray, and they draped the material on the walls.

"Whoever dropped these bolts off, it's ideal for this occasion."

"Who knew the Lord worked in fabric."

"Betsy, He also works on wedding receptions. The material will work for Douglas and mine too. Do you realize we'll be husband and wife in less than two months? And we both appreciate what y'all have done for us. Especially bringing us together."

"In you and your daughter's case, we couldn't help but play Cupid. You're just too cute together…all three of you."

The young woman's cheeks changed to a light shade of pink. "Under no circumstances did I imagine finding a man who adored Olivia and me as much as Douglas does."

"Amen. You snatched a good one. Now back to the task at hand. Any ideas on what we can use to cover the circular table? The tops of most of them are scratched and are not screaming romance."

"Rose, why don't we use the off-white lace tablecloth I put away the other day?" Betsy found it in the cabinet now hidden behind the folds of fabric. "Oh, and here's a bunch of dark gray candles. A centerpiece which goes with our décor."

"And they match everything. Thank you, Lord!" Rose draped the tablecloth on the table and evened the edges. Then she plopped into a chair. "I'm resting for a minute before I go home to prepare a prime rib someone said I was cooking."

"What about the food we're going to serve with the side of beef I ordered?" Betsy winked at Everly.

"Oh my goodness. We forgot about—"

Betsy observed her friend's frantic search for her phone and intervened. "Our hubbies are washing potatoes as we speak."

"Glory Hallelujah. Bets, you're the best. We are working our magic once again."

"Go home. I'll lock up." Everly tucked the empty bolts under her arm, and the three left the room.

CHAPTER NINE

Despite Dillon's presence at the second-hand store the following day, the surprise dinner remained a secret. However, she raised an eyebrow when Rose tried to coax her to the women's side of the shop at the end of the day by saying, "I have an outfit to show you."

"I have more than enough clothes. The places I've called on don't have enough closets to hang what I do have. I'll have to use the extra bedroom for storage instead of an office. Give the clothing to someone in the program." Dillon resumed rolling men's socks.

"Dear, it's adorable." Betsy steered the two women around racks of men's clothing. And getting them to the other side of the building meant she'd be able to answer her editor's text. He waited in the parking lot of the adjacent building. "Dillon, this outfit – it is you. Go. Go. Go."

Rose gave a thumbs-up behind her back as they strolled into the lady's section of Sassy Seconds *Two*. Betsy waited until they were gone, and she called Andrew. "Coast is clear, but don't move. I'm coming to you."

She semi-raced/limped to her editor. "Hello, Andrew. We don't have time for chit-chat. Rosie is stalling Dillon, so we have to get you inside without her seeing you. Think you can do that?" Betsy's comment came out a little snappier than she had planned. "Sorry."

"I deserve all the abuse you throw at me. Dillon is going to kill—"

"There's a good chance you're correct, but have faith. We're praying for you. Let's get moving."

They made it to the fitting room without detection, and Betsy heard, "It's perfect," from Andrew, who stood behind her. "It is, and whatever charm you have locked inside your six-foot frame, you better pull it out. You have to keep her from walking out on you again."

"Yes, I do." Andrew pulled out a chair and sat. "How much time do I have before Dillon arrives?"

"Around twenty minutes or so. Sit tight while I keep an eye out for them."

Betsy waited at the door, and her editor's question hit her. And to add brevity to the situation, she said, "Since Dillon doesn't know you're here, she hasn't hired a hitman to take you out. But she may have one on speed dial."

"Betsy, I know I screwed up."

"You certainly did." She faced the young man. "But we all do crazy things, but what you pulled...I haven't thought of a word to describe it yet. However, it's fixable. I'd suggest, if you're not a praying man, become one." Betsy spotted Rose. "I'll be back."

She hobbled to her friend to find out their next step but spotted Dillon in her new outfit. A compliment stayed on Betsy's lips when Rose blurted out, "The yellow flowers in the sundress make your tan look even better. And the sandals are keepers too."

"And I'm still stumped as to why you wanted me to leave this on. All I'm doing is going to the hotel and write."

"There's been a change of pla—" The last word caught in Betsy's throat at the sight of Ben and Larry. They carried dinner plates in, and the smell of prime rib wafted in the air for all of Lee County to savor.

Dillon turned her attention toward the door. "Whatever you have smells delicious, but my plans haven't changed. Chapter Twenty-Two is waiting for me to finish. Bryce and Alexis are about to get together."

"Let me explain."

"Rosie, I've heard about your matchmaking, but I'm not interested in whoever you have in there waiting for me."

Andrew came out of the fitting room. "Dillon, it's me."

"What are you doing here?" The mystery author covered her face. "Why, after all these years?"

"When I saw you at the conference in Daytona, I realized how much I still loved you. I blew an opportunity years ago to win you back, but I'm not going to let you go without a fight this time."

"Well, wearing underwear on your head probably wasn't the best way to convince her."

Everyone in the room gasped at Rosie's whispered words, and Betsy prayed Dillon had lost her hearing. She hadn't. And her next words, she yelled loud enough for Bonita Springs to hear. "It was you?"

"I can explain."

"Dillon and Andrew, come on in here and take your seats." Rose scurried to the table. "We've decorated it all pretty for you two. It's the ideal place to discuss your differences. Are you ready for your salads?"

"No, but I'm curious why he thought scaring me half to death would persuade me to change my mind." Dillon's fists stayed at her side, and her eyes clamped down on Betsy then Rose. "Did you call him after I shared my heart with you?"

"Not exactly." Betsy searched her mind for the right words to say to her friend.

"Yes, Bets called, but I prompted her to do it after I put the puzzle pieces together. We solved the mystery of the disappearing man. Now, can you sit down and listen to the poor man who—"

"Who wants to explain himself if Rosie will zip it shut and go into the other room?" Betsy's tone of voice must have put a pep in everyone's steps. Rose disappeared out the side door, and Ben and Larry followed after they sat the food on the table.

Bets stayed behind to take the lids off the food. As she removed the last one, she said, "Eat while the meal is hot. It'll go down better while you're discussing." She exited the room, but only around the corner. There she'd be able to listen to her editor's tale.

"Dillon, please hear me out. And, yes, I'm stupid for playing dead. But it accomplished what I had set out to do – to get your attention. I love you. And always have."

"No doubt, it got my attention, but not in a good way. You can't expect me to believe you still love me. Get serious." Dillon scooted her chair back. "And the way you picked to show your love. Priceless."

"Not my brightest moment, but I've never been more serious. I love you and want you to give us another chance."

Silence filled the room after his heartfelt plea, but the stillness carried on longer than Betsy liked. She stole a glance into the open door. *Should I interrupt them, Lord, or let them hash it out.* She waited for a prompting, but nothing. She tried again. *Father, yoohoo, awake up up there—*

"Since you're not talking, I'll expound on my idiocy. On a whim, I asked Arlene where you were camping. Once I found out, I planned to do the stunt, wait a day, and then I'd come clean. I thought we'd have a good laugh."

"Do you see me laughing?"

"I don't, but there was another motive to my madness. You'd said in one of your classes at the conference that you were dealing with writer's block. I wanted to help you conquer the mountain. Arlene and—"

"Funny you'd mention Arlene. She and her cousins had the same idea. Thanks to all of you for attempting to jump-start my writing career, but I cannot put my head around how any of you thought this was a good idea."

"Dillon, this is where it gets tricky. Your agent, her cousins, and I agreed to work together. They only scattered the notes, per Detective Wilds, but they had no clue about my showing up in the laundry room as a dead man, but…"

"But what, Andrew? How did you actually pull it off without anyone seeing you?"

"It wasn't easy. I pitched a tent, not too far from your site, and stayed awake. Didn't want to miss when you headed to the showers."

"How'd you know I wouldn't use the one in the RV?"

"Dillon, I've seen their bathrooms. They're small. I went with my gut that you'd use the facility in the campground, and I was right

"You realize stalking a person is a crime?"

"I do, and I'm sorry." Andrew reached for his glass of tea. "Dillon, I'm sorry for so many things."

"I don't want to hear it, but Arlene's cousin, who is working on my case, might be interested."

"Betsy gave me his phone number. I'll call him tomorrow. I should have cleared it up and not wasted his time."

"I don't know if Wilds will bring charges against you for fabricating a crime, but I'm sure he's as anxious to put this behind him as I am. Even without your stunt, I planned to call the police about the notes when I returned to New York. But then you showed up, which…"

"Which scared you. Please forgive me. "Trust me, Arlene and I knew nothing about what the other intended, but I'll bet you've written three-quarters of your next book because of what we did. Am I right?"

"And all it took was you putting a pair of underwear on your head and holding a musical instrument."

Betsy couldn't see Dillon's expression, but Andrew's held promise. At least the famous author hadn't thrown her sweet tea at him. *And, Mr. Pickle, this is a good time for you to reiterate how you feel about her.*

"Dillon, I'll say it again. I'm so sorry I frightened you. The stunt with the underwear was a last-minute decision. I didn't want you to recognize me."

"Not a chance of me knowing it was you under your disguise."

"I had another reason to do it besides helping to kick start your writing" Andrew jumped out of his chair and knelt next to her. "As I've said, I've never stopped loving you, and I want to spend the rest of my life—"

"No! No! And No! This is too much." Dillon rose from her chair with such force it slammed against the wall. "I appreciate your help with my writing, but our relationship died years ago. Goodbye, Andrew."

Betsy hid behind the door with her feet glued to the floor until Dillon disappeared into the next room, and the door slammed. She snuck a peek at Andrew and found him in his chair. His chin rested on his chest, and her pleas to Heaven started.

"I know you're out there. What do you propose I do now?"

Betsy's prayer ended when she heard Andrew's question. And she took it as an invitation to reenter the room. "My advice is to chase her down. Find out why she's so scared of commitment. Cold feet is fear of the unknown. Go now."

Her editor bolted out the same door Dillon had exited. A minute later, he returned. "Rosie caught me. She told me to leave her alone for the time being. Betsy, I've gone and done it again."

"She can't run forever."

"Betsy, she's done it for ten years. Why stop now?" Andrew's shoulders slumped as he made his way to the back door. When he reached his destination, he turned and said, "Thank you for your help, but it appears pretty hopeless at this point."

~~~

Bets left Dillon alone over the weekend. However, on Monday morning, she called her. The topic of Andrew Pickle stayed on the forbidden list—until a slip in judgment fell out of Betsy's mouth, "Your life can have a happy ending…like your books."

"They're fiction. Reality doesn't always turn out

rosy."

"Sounds like someone needs to talk about it?"

"Not really."

"Alrighty then. If you do, you know where I am. Talk to you soon." Betsy clicked off her phone and wheeled the donation cart with laundered and ironed items to the women's section. Her phone buzzed. *'Everly and I are going to her dress fitting. We'll be in by noonish.'*

Betsy spent the next three hours hanging clothes on their coordinating racks. Thank goodness for air conditioning because temperatures hovered around ninety-four in mid-September. "If I planned a wedding, it'd be in December or January."

"Have you forgotten you're already married?" Ben's voice startled her.

"If I ever dump you, those are the months I'm swaying towards for Husband #Two." Bets snuggled up next to her hubby. "But you're a keeper. Oh, and thanks for helping us with the dinner the other night, but it may be all for naught. Dillon isn't in the mood to talk."

"Give her time. Can you imagine the shock of finding out what Andrew did, and then he tells her he loves her? That took guts."

"True love. He held a torch for her all these years. How romantic." Betsy placed her hands on her heart then gave Ben a tender kiss on his cheek. "I lov—" She cut off the last word when she saw Dillon standing in the doorway. *Oh, we're in such deep trouble.*

The mystery writer marched up to them. "Can we get off the subject of romance and get these clothes put away?"

"We sure can. Hon, I'm out of here." Ben rushed into the next room.

"So, Dillon, how long were you listening to our jabbering?"

"Long enough to hear you discussing Andrew's and my behavior, which is no one's business." The author snatched the handle of the cart next to Betsy. "I'll finish hanging these clothes."

"Don't get too involved." Rose entered the room. "I'll go get us Taco Bell for lunch. That is when I find my keys." She searched her pockets. "Have you seen them?"

"Nope, but it sounds yummy." Betsy retrieved another cart and left Dillon alone. While she sorted clothes by color, she prayed. *Lord, give us the words to help her and Andrew. And, please help us to tone down on our rambunctiousness. We don't want to scare her away.*

Betsy closed out her prayer, and at that moment, she spied a read-a-newspaper-through-it tank top. She wheeled her cart next to Dillon. "I do not see 'Dress for Success' written on this number. You?" Betsy twirled it in the air and silently thanked the Lord for His sense of humor.

The writer's laughter, and shaking head, let Bets know the flimsy camisole belonged in the trash. Along with another item on her cart. She held up a pair of shorts, measuring six inches from waistband to jagged hem. "A definite no to this one too" Betsy lay it in the trash pile.

"I don't want to know where Rose finds these…these…I don't have a name for them."

"It appears she needs supervision again if she's visiting places where these are the norm," Betsy shared the story about Rose buying gift cards at Cantaloupe's on their travels up the east coast.

"Isn't it a place similar to Hooters—"

"Yep. And Rosie planned to go back and give the cards to a man standing on the street corner she'd met earlier," With each word Betsy spoke, tears started to roll down Dillon's cheeks.

"You cannot be serious?"

"I am. And if I'd had my phone ready when Rose shared it with us, the video would have gone viral." Betsy wiped her tears on the tank and handed it to Dillon. "Here, use this. We're out of tissues."

"Thanks for finding a way to lighten my mood." Dillon dabbed at her eyes then fingered the see-through number once more as if she inspected every thread. After a bit, she tossed it in the trash can. "And, thank you for not getting angry at my grumpiness."

"We threw way too much stuff at you Friday night. If you're anything like me – I'm not fond of surprises."

"I'm a fan of surprises, but finding out Andrew was responsible for scaring me then shares he still loves me – it's a bit too much to handle." Dillon fumbled with a jacket zipper. "Betsy, I have my career. It's everything I ever wanted."

This time when the tears fell, Betsy knew no amount of humor would solve her problem. *Please, Lord, be with me. I'm going off the high board.* "Dillon, let's take a walk."

"You better leave a note for Rose to tell her where to bring our lunch."

"Smart girl."

As always, the humid air hit Betsy when she opened the door. They walked in silence to the picnic table behind the store. "Let's sit here. It's cooler."

The live oak limbs gave shade on the table Ben and Larry built. They sat at it when the weather cooled in

January and February, but Bets came out and used it as a desk on occasion when she needed to get away from people.

"Betsy, nothing you or Rose can say will change my mind. I'm content with my life."

"Dillon, please excuse my forthrightness, but you're full of beans. You aren't content. You tell yourself you're pleased with how your career is going. When in truth, you're paddling to reach the edge, but the water is covering your head."

"Ouch."

"Sorry, but you're not experiencing contentment. My guess, it's fear of commitment. In Ben's and my situation, our relationship teetered on the edge when writing became more important to me than he was. My advice – listen to what the Lord is telling you, Dillon."

Betsy finished and expected her friend to walk away. But she stayed. However, the unfinished hem of her denim skirt became her focal point. If Bets didn't stop her, Dillon would unravel the entire thi—.

"I haven't listened to Him in a long time, and it's obvious when I resort to begging a total stranger to take me in the RV. Then we can add in all the mayhem since we left the conference. And, now a long-lost beau of mine shows up, and I have a meltdown for all to see."

"No one begged anyone. Dillon, we invited you. And it's why you came along—to acquire friends like us. We can handle breakdowns. Rose has one at least once a week."

"I do not. Don't listen to Betsy." Rosie countered as she and Everly joined them at the picnic table. They carried shopping bags and a Taco Bell sack. "Let's eat."

Everly unwrapped her taco and appeared to study it.

After a while, everyone quit chewing and peered at the young woman. Her skin took on an ashen tone, and sweat beaded on her forehead. And she hadn't taken a bite of any spiciness yet.

"Please share with us what the taco is telling you?" Betsy tossed out witticism, hoping to jar Everly out of her head.

"It's telling me I shouldn't get married and saddle Douglas with a teenager." Everly burst into tears. "He will regret it."

Dillon rose from her seat. "How about we take the afternoon off? Girl time and chatting are good for the soul."

"What a brilliant idea. Bets and I can handle the shop. And if she doesn't quit kicking me under the table, I'll send her with you. Go!"

"Thank you." Everly wiped her tears. "Dillon, don't you have a book to finish? It's much more important than me and my problems."

"No, it's not. My writing can wait. Anyway, it helps to talk to a friend when you're having trouble. Come on. Let's get going." Dillon winked at Betsy. "We'll see you ladies in the morning."

"Bye." Betsy's supreme nachos remained in the cardboard box, holding little appeal after Everly's announcement. *Was she getting cold feet? What about the wedding? What if Dillon tries to talk her out of marrying Douglas?* "There's no way. She wouldn't. Would she?"

"Betsy, you're talking out loud, and you're thinking what I'm thinking. We have to stop our dear writer friend." Rose attempted to get her short legs over the picnic bench, but it soon resembled a seal stuck on a sand bar.

"Halt what you're doing. And Rosebud, I'm saying this to both of us. 'Trust in the Lord with all your heart and lean not on your own understanding; in all your ways submit to him and he will make your paths straight.'"

"And if you're finished quoting verses, we have to go after them." Rose's second try to leave the picnic table accomplished getting one leg over. The other dangled five inches off the cement. "Help."

Betsy muffled her merriment to assist in her friend's predicament. "Short legs are pesky. And we're not going anywhere. Even if I questioned Dillon's motive for a moment, I'm trusting the Lord on this. Our writer friend is not talking Everly out of marrying Dou—"

"Douglas, you're right on time." Rose patted the seat next to her. "Sit. Tell Bets and me how the wedding plans are going."

"Other than my knee in a brace, which I pray will be removed in a month, everything's great. Everly's daughter and her Aunt Mildred have become my shadows. I hope they're giving my fiancé as much attention as they are me."

"They're…ah…spreading it…around." Betsy's hesitant rambling filled the air.

"I'm glad they're not ignoring her. By the way, do you know where my soon-to-be bride is hiding?"

As if on cue, Rose and Betsy made a gagging noise at Douglas's question. He reached inside his little cooler, sitting next to him, and brought out a bottle of water for each of them. "I have more if you need them."

Bets took a long drink, and after swallowing, said, "Thank you. I hate when a tortilla gets stuck in my throat."

"Back to my question. Have you seen Everly? We are tasting cakes this afternoon at 4:00, and it's at the bakery across town."

All speech left Betsy, but she managed to give Douglas a blank stare. Rose matched her deer-in-the-headlight look from across the picnic table. *Lord, words from any of us right now would be appreciated. Anything!*

"It's okay, you two. It's obvious you're hiding something from me. I love surprises." Douglas rose from the table. "For a minute, I thought you were going to tell me she'd changed her mind."

Rose found her voice and squeaked out, "Now that's funny."

"It is, and I guess I better get to work." He walked across the parking lot and entered the side door of the store.

The door closed, and Betsy rubbed her forehead—for a long time then said, "This morning I spoke into the mirror, 'Stay home. Write all day. Rose, Everly, and Dillon will take care of the shop.' But, no. I came to work and have witnessed my own soap opera."

"And it's called: Early Birds Conquer Cold Feet. And, as much as I hate to say this, we can't fix this. We have to get the two men involved. Yes, we can do our part, but Douglas and Andrew have to go in front of the women they love and plead their cases. But first, we have to pray."

She listened to Rose, and per her usual, she got a little wordy. Bets interrupted her and said, 'AMEN!'"

"I cannot believe you butted in. The best part of my prayer was coming where I'd remind the Lord He had the power to shut the lion's mouth."

"He's already aware of His abilities, but it is funny. I must possess His power 'cause I just shut your mouth." Betsy snickered.

"Oh, you're soooo amusing." Rose handed Betsy her phone. "I'll go and find Douglas, because Everly has probably called by now. Your assignment is to text Andrew and tell him to get over here. We have to nip this in the bud. Two ladies are awaiting their happily ever afters."

CHAPTER TEN

Andrew showed up near closing time, but Dillon refused to see him. Everly avoided Douglas too. Both ladies busied themselves behind the counter. At one point, the mystery writer stated, "We're not interested in what they have to say. We have work to do."

"Ditto," Everly's voice echoed in agreement.

"How about we move to the picnic table out of earshot?" The four sat down, and Betsy continued. "I'd say this attempt fizzled, but let's not give up." She got on her phone and Googled romantic gifts. Diamonds, round-the-world cruises, and prices to fly to Paris for a week popped up. "Guys, I don't know what your budget is, but from what I'm seeing – you need to up it."

Betsy shared what she'd seen on the internet, and the men agreed their budgets, together, wouldn't pay for one of the gifts.

"And, from what I remember, Dillon's requirement in life is her computer, a quiet place to write, and words flowing out of her fingers. Simplicity. It's hard for a man to compete. And she's big on honesty too."

"If you want her in your life again, you'll have to

figure it out. Hey, I think I have it. Since she loves the written word, write her a love letter. Be honest and vulnerable – if that's what she is looking for."

"Good idea, Rosie."

"Everly is more of an old movie buff. She'll fix bags of popcorn, and we'll all snuggle on the couch for hours on the weekend."

"We're onto something, Douglas. Go and watch a dozen romantic movies." Betsy Googled 1950/1960s movies. "Find out what Cary Grant said to his love interest to persuade them to fall in love with him?"

"I'll do it, but remind me again who this Grant guy is. He sounds familiar."

Betsy showed him a studio shot from 1963. "He's definitely before your time, but you'd do well to mimic a person who dresses as tasteful as he did. And he drips sophistication with the way he talks."

"Oh, how she digresses. Douglas, as Betsy said, polish your debonairedness. Andrew, get to writing your love note. And while you're at it – it can't hurt to throw in a bouquet of their favorite flo ."

"Ladies, Larry and I have listened to your malarkey long enough. If the Lord wants these four to get married. He'll take care of the incidentals. Our advice – be yourselves…and pray and listen for His answer."

~~~

A week and a half later, Dillon and Everly's happily ever after seemed as far away as Savannah was to Switzerland. "If you have a Plan Z, please tell me now. We've exhausted A through Y. How do parents do it with unruly children? I'll guarantee this is how it must feel."

"No doubt, Betsy. And we're down to the wire. We

have—" Rose cut off her sentence when Everly entered the room, then added. "Dear, how is your day going?"

"If canceling the church tells you anything, I'm not doing well."

"You what?" Betsy's response came out faster than planned. "Sorry, but why? You two have to get married. You love Douglas, and he loves you."

"Too many risks." Everly gathered a folded pile of clothing in her arms and made it to the door. "My mind is made up. I told Douglas this morning." The young woman escaped into the next room.

"Betsy, meteorologists say when they run out of people's names, they start naming storms with the Greek alphabet. Today, we've reached Alpha and Omega." Rose crossed her arms. "And it's all I've got. You have anything?"

"Nothing. It's time for an Early Birds meeting. I'll text Ben to get the guys over here. I'm checking with Dillon too. See what her schedule is. I'd rather she not come in while we're discussing ideas concerning her and Andrew. Didn't bode well the last time."

"Good idea."

Within seconds, her phone buzzed twice. "Ben and Larry are on their way. And Dillon won't be in until later in the d—"

"We're here. Where do you want us?" Ben approached them. Larry followed close behind.

"At the picnic table." Betsy took her seat next to her hubby. "If you haven't heard, Everly has cancelled the church. I've also talked to Dillon to clear up the question we all have – she told me she is NOT trying to talk Everly out of getting married. In fact, she's emphatic she go ahead with it."

"Did she say anything about Andrew and her working on their relationship?"

"Rosebud, rabbit trails are for another time. Get back to the topic at hand." Larry took a drink of water.

"This has always been a serious situation, but her cancelling the church puts it over the top." Bets lifted her hand and moved it side to side. "This is me waving the white flag. Rose and I have exhausted all our ideas. You're next."

"How about the four of us have a chat with Douglas and Andrew. We can share the fine art of marriage with them, having survived the rigors of matrimony ourselves and lived to tell the tale. Benjamin, are you with me?"

"Larry Wilford, you may be onto something."

"I've texted Andrew, and he said he's free after 6:00. So, when he gets here, we'll hide him in the backroom and have Douglas meet us there."

"Rosie, I'll keep Everly busy in the front of the store. When it's time to close the shop, I'll make some excuse as to why she has to walk around the building to get to her car."

"Outstanding. DEFCOM – we ready to…to…shootypoop…what do they do with bombs?"

"Rosie, they launch them."

"Why isn't it a more dramatic name for what they do?"

"Everyone, ignore my wife. Our plan will *launch* at 1800 hours. See you inside."

~~~

Betsy had witnessed a firing squad in movies, but these two young men's wider-than-normal eyes gave the impression they'd see one in the next little while. "Relax. We're not going to bite, judge, or harm you in any way.

We are here to help you. Ben, you're up."

"Let's start with prayer. None of this will have any lasting effects unless we bring Him into it." Ben bowed his head. "Lord, open our hearts to hear You. Help all of us to speak Your words to these men. And everybody said, 'AMEN!'"

"Amen. And I brought water in case anyone wants one." Betsy held a bottle in each hand.

"Are we going to baptize them when we're finished talking to them?"

"Lar, we only do that on job sights." Ben chuckled. "On second thought, you better give me a water." When Betsy gave it to him, he unscrewed the lid and held it. "Hope you don't mind, but I've changed the format. Douglas, if you want to get married, you'll have to convince her you're the man."

"She had grasped this fact until Dillon McCloud came into our lives and gave her a spiel about cold feet."

Betsy handed Douglas a bottle of water. "Dillon isn't here to defend herself, but trust me, she's doing everything to encourage Everly to marry you. Your fiancé's fears from the past are the issue here. Now it's your turn to reassure her."

"How, other than kidnapping her on November twentieth?"

"Strive to come up with another workable option – not one where you'd spend your honeymoon in jail." Rose pointed out the striped shirt she had on. "Douglas, don't consider committing a crime. Wearing stripes or orange jumpsuits is no one's friend."

"Since Rosie likes to steer us in a different direction, I'll bring us back to topic. Again. Douglas, Everly needs to know you're not going anywhere. You are marrying her for better or worse. And you love her daughter Olivia as your own."

"I adore both of them…with all my heart."

"We know you do. Now you have to reassure Everly she's your one and only." Rose turned to Andrew. "And Mr. Pickle, we haven't heard from you. Are you awake?"

The editor jumped. "This is about Douglas. There's no hope for Dillon and me."

"Son, there's always hope."

"You sound like my dad."

"Apparently, you didn't listen to him either if you're still clinging to hopelessness." Ben proceeded to drain his water bottle then added, "What's eating at you?"

"You won't like what I have to say."

"Try us. Nothing you say will shock or surprise us."

"I have my doubts. Your opinion of me will change. And it's why Dillon wants nothing to do with me." Andrew leaned back in his chair. "She gave you her go-to phrase about getting cold feet. Truth is an old girlfriend called me a week before the wedding, and I went to mee—"

"Did God give you a brain of mush?" Rose's cheeks switched from flesh-colored to beet red in seconds, and she wagged her finger in his direction. "No one goes running—"

"Rosebud, sit down. Andrew, you have the floor."

"I went to meet Suzanne, my old girlfriend. She'd called and asked me to meet her at a hotel. The minute I saw her, I knew I'd screwed up and got the heck out of there as fast as my wheels would take me. Dillon found out about it, and she refused to give me a chance to explain.

"I don't mean to make light of your situation, but this

is going to take a lot more than flowers." Larry draped his arm on the back of his wife's chair.

"Let the man continue, so we know what to pray for."

"I need more than prayers. And I have sent flowers, along with cards, singing telegrams, and—"

"We can't forget about when you played dead," Betsy added in his latest escapade, hoping he recognized his choices needed work.

"It rates as my worst idea to date, but nothing I said or gifts I've sent changed her mind. And the note Suzanne sent to Dillon sealed it. Lies on top of lies. I was wrong. Please help me figure out how to win her trust back. I'll do anything."

"Anything?" Dillon snuck around the corner and leaned against the door jamb. "Andrew, it'll be tough to top wearing frilly underwear, but if you put a pair on in front of my friends – I'll reconsider how to handle your prank."

Everly tiptoed into the room, wearing a big smile. "Hope it's okay that we eavesdropped on your meeting. But your suggestion I use the front door made me suspicious. The final straw—Douglas texting me. Continuously. Can't a girl have any peace while she's planning her wedding?"

"What?"

"Douglas, if you will have me, the wedding is on…if you all will agree to have the weddings and reception at Sassy Seconds *Two?*"

Andrew leaped from his chair. "Weddings? Who else is getting married?"

Tears streaked Everly's cheeks. "Dillon will have to answer that question, but first – Douglas, will you marry me on November twentieth like we planned and make me the happiest woman on the planet?"

"It's either you marry me, or I'm flying to the far reaches of Africa. Oh, I can't. I'm afraid of flying. Everly, the answer is YES!" They left the room, acting as if no one else existed in the world.

"Now, who else is getting hitched?"

"Andrew Pickle, we'll get back to the discussion of marriage in a bit." Dillon crossed her arms. "But first, I am curious about a note we found at the campground. Arlene said they planted them, but the one that said, 'Words written on a page aren't always the truth' sounded familiar."

"I'd written the words in a text after you read Suzanne's letter. I was telling you then, and now, don't believe everything you read, especially Suzanne. Please forgive me, Dillon. I never meant to hurt you."

"You did, but I should have heard you out. I'm sorry." She smiled. "So, about marrying…"

Andrew dropped to one knee in front of Dillon. "I'll take it from here. Will you marry me?"

"Most definitely." She leaned in and gave Andrew a lingering kiss.

Betsy shooed everyone out of the room. "Privacy, people."

"Let's not move too far. I'm all ears for the rest of the story." Rosie inched closer to the door, and the others followed.

"Lucky for you, Mr. Pickle, I broke up with Thomas two months ago. He wasn't the one, and I realized it at the conference. Anyway, he was gone way too much. My hope is you will be home for dinner more than once a year."

"So, you'll give us another chance?"

"Can I have my own office wherever we live?"

"Ms. McCloud, you can have anything your heart desires. We can also wait and get married at the Biltmore if you want. It's your choice. I'll wait."

"Well, that's the sweetest thing I've ever witnessed in my sixty-plus years on earth." Rose stepped from the shadows. "It's another praise the Lord, and pass the turtle soup time."

"Are we having turtle soup again?" Andrew Pickle looked in the direction of the empty table.

"No!" Four voices rang out in the fitting room at Sassy Seconds *Two*.

EPILOGUE

Everly and Dillon dressed in their gowns and waited for their weddings to begin. Betsy and Aunt Mildred fussed with the women's trains, making them ready for the young women's journey to meet their future husbands.

Betsy stepped back. "If I haven't told you before, you two are stunning. *Bride's* magazine should feature a photograph of both of you." She dabbed at her eyes. "And don't make me cry on the only day I've worn makeup in five years."

"We'd never think of it." Dillon smiled, and her eyes glistened.

"Can I scoot in here?" Arlene handed Dillon her bouquet. "I'm glad you quit being mad at me and invited me to your big day. You two are gorgeous. And I'm glad you and Andrew found your way back to each other."

"Be quiet. Now you're going to make me cry." Dillon blinked. "I won't cry. I'm happy, happy, happy." She smiled at Arlene. "Anyhoo, how could I stay mad at my agent, who always looks out for my best interest? Sometimes in weird ways. How are your cousins?"

"Detective Wilds closed the case, and Florence is

back at the campground. She promised them she'd curtail any antics in the future. By the way, I have a taker for your next book—"

The door flew open, stopping her conversation. All eyes centered on Betsy's mom. "I can check on the brisket later, but I had to come to see Dillon and Everly's dresses. Turn around. Now I have to run." She flitted to the door, and on her way out, she added, "They are breathtaking."

The brides' exquisite yet different dresses expressed the two young women's tastes. Elegant, yet unassuming. And they'd scoured every bridal store in Southwest Florida to find Dillon's idyllic gown.

"I don't know where Rose is, but please convey this message to her. Thank you both for all you've done." Dillon brushed at the side of her eye. "And, Everly, my new best friend, thank you for sharing your day with a couple you met a few months ago. It's such a God thing."

Rose popped her head around the corner. "He knew what He was doing when He brought these four together. Oh, and Everly, it's time for you to see your daughter. Olivia, come in and model.

The fifteen-year-old entered the room to oohs and aahs. Dillon had somehow transformed the bolts of gray chiffon they'd used at the matchmaking dinner into a flowing gown with spaghetti straps for Olivia. The tulip hem touched her mid-calf.

"You are exquisite…and all grown up." Everly's lashes brimmed with tears.

"Mom, don't you dare cry. Your mascara will run." Olivia handed her mom a tissue then faced Dillon. "Ms. McCloud, thank you for my dress. I'm wearing it to prom – if I have a date or not."

"You'll have boys standing in line to ask you out."

"Rose, I'd prefer she not date until she's in her mid-thirties."

"Like you, Mom? But Daddy Doug was worth the wait."

A chorus of "Amens" rang through the room. "You have a smart child." Betsy pushed a curl behind Olivia's ear then peeked out through the blind. "Ben is standing at the door. Mildred, he will take you to your seat." As she relayed the message, the music started. "That's our cue."

Ben opened the door and offered his arm to Everly's aunt. Betsy teared up as her hubby walked the woman down the aisle. Once he seated her, Everly and her daughter began their march to the sound of "Over the Rainbow." The light and airy melody filled the warehouse.

The tune finished, and an Etta James song began. "At Last" accompanied Dillon, Betsy, and Rose down the aisle. The mystery writer insisted they'd both join her. 'You two are responsible for bringing Andrew and me together…again.'"

They made it to the front, and the dual ceremony began. Everly and Douglas selected traditional vows and repeated the words the pastor spoke. Near the end, he asked, "Is there anyone who objects to the union of these two people? Speak now or forever hold your peace."

Everly's daughter moved closer to Douglas and whispered loud enough for all to hear, "Dad, I'm not objecting, but I forgot to ask you something. Will you adopt me after you marry Mom?"

If a man could beam, his face shone like the noonday sun. He kissed her on her forehead. "Olivia, I'd be honored." Then, after the cheering from the wedding party stopped, he turned to the pastor. "You can proceed."

"If you're wondering what happened up here. Olivia asked Douglas to adopt her. He—" The audience drowned out his words with clapping and congratulations. The pastor put up his hand. "We approved too. And Everly and Douglas, I suggest you go to the courthouse on Monday, but for now, I pronounce you husband and wife. You may kiss the bride."

The couple kissed, and the people in attendance cheered for a second time. Afterward, Everly, Douglas, and Olivia marched up the aisle, arm in arm.

The pastor motioned for Andrew and Dillon to step forward. "These two are making my life simpler today. They've written their vows. Andrew, you may begin."

"Dillon, I've loved you from our first date and have kicked myself every day for messing up our happily ever after. But we're here today. Thank you for forgiving me and giving me another chance.

"Andrew, I love you too. Meeting Betsy and Rose, and RVing with them, changed my life and brought us back together. All I can say – I can't wait until our children grow up so I can tell them the wacky way their parents reconnected. Thank you for loving me, even at my worst."

The pastor opened his Bible, and Dillon and Andrew exchanged their rings. "And now, Andrew and Dillon, I pronounce you husband and wife. You, too, may kiss your bride."

"Finally. Oh, I'm not supposed to use 'ly' words."

"Andrew, be quiet and kiss me."

He did, and the audience hollered one more time. The

wedding party then progressed up the aisle for the reception in the main showroom of Sassy Seconds *Two*. The evening included pictures, hors d'oeuvres, cupcakes with frosting and sprinkles, and hugs galore.

Around 9:30, the newly married couples walked over to the Early Birds. Everly spoke first, "I've said it a dozen times, but thank you for EVERYTHING. We're together because of all of you."

"She's going to make me cry, and I agree with what Everly said." Dillon nudged her hubby and said. "And, Rose and Betsy, the next RV trip we take together, you'll have to find a bed for Andrew so he can come along. The Biltmore is waiting."

"How does speaking at the North Carolina Christian Writers Conference sound? I posted that we were getting married, and they asked us to come next year. The facility is a short distance away from Asheville."

"I'm in."

"Dillon, maybe Everly and I will purchase an RV. We can tag along with the Early Birds when it's slow at the second-hand store. What do you think?"

"Yes! Yes! And Yes!" Rosie wiped a tear. "Betsy, we may not have had kids of our own, but these four are our children from another mother and father. Thank You, Lord, for Your many blessings."

"Amen!" The Early Birds answered as one.

BIO:
Turning Life into Comedy is Janetta Fudge Messmer's tagline. She loves to laugh, and it's why she writes Christian Comedy (with a touch of Romance). For Janetta, writing and traveling go hand in hand since she, her hubby (Ray), and their pooch (Maggie) are full-time RVers. Most days, you'll find them out sightseeing…but first Janetta has to sit down and write a few words.

JANETTA'S INFORMATION:

Janetta Fudge Messmer
"Turning Life into Comedy"
Author of Christian Comedies (with a touch of Romance).
My books are available on
Amazon: https://www.amazon.com/-/e/B01DWHA1EW
E-mail: janettafudgemessmer@gmail.com
Website: http://janettafudgemessmer.com/
Facebook: https://www.facebook.com/janetta.fudge.messmer
Twitter: https://twitter.com/nettiefudge

IT'S A MYSTERY...BIRDS

www.ingramcontent.com/pod-product-compliance
Lightning Source LLC
LaVergne TN
LVHW010325070526
838199LV00065B/5656